CARVING OUT A FUTURE

LARCHDOWN VALLEY
BOOK THREE

JEM WENDEL

Published by Larking About Press

ISBN: 978-1-916758-06-3 (ebook edition)

ISBN: 978-1-916758-07-0 (Paperback edition)

First edition v1.1, February 2024

Edited by Jenn Green - https://www.jennreadsmmbooks.com/

Proofread by SJ Buckley - https://www.sjbuckley-editingandproofreading.com

Carving out a Future

Jem Wendel

CONTENT WARNINGS

AUTHOR'S NOTE

This book is written in British English. There are spelling differences between British and US English so please take this into account when reading.

There will also be phrases that are unique to the UK and may seem unfamiliar. If you have any concerns or questions please reach out to the author on their social media channels.

PART I
SPRING

CHAPTER 1

 uncan

I GAZE UP at the sign, *The Blacksmith's Arms*. It's the first English pub I've seen in over fifteen years. If I've ever thought of what a quintessential pub in a typical English village looks like, this is definitely what comes to mind. With its thatched roof and leaded windows, it's real chocolate box stuff, and a far cry from the steel and concrete I usually see all day.

I turn and look round, across the village green at the lush, verdant environment—from a weeping willow heading down towards a riverbank, quaint cottages and shops making up the village, to the sweeping hills and woods beyond. Spring is starting to show its glory, and I can't quite believe that only thirty-six hours ago I was leaving my apartment in Sydney. I wonder, not for the first time, if I'm doing the right thing in coming here.

What does he think of me? Will he want to see me? If he

doesn't want to, then at least I'll know for sure. I can't really blame him. He probably thinks I abandoned him all those years ago, but it wasn't like that at all. I could've been in touch sooner, but he was always very much in his brother's shadow. It was clear what David, my eldest son, thought of me and my lifestyle. But when word reached me that my youngest son had got engaged—and to whom—I hoped that his brother's influence might not be so far-reaching. So here I am, back in my home country and about to gatecrash my own son's wedding.

THE INTERIOR of the pub is dark, and it takes a few minutes for my eyes to adjust to the low light.

"Can I help you?"

I turn towards the source of the voice and see a short, dark-haired woman standing at the end of the bar.

"I have a reservation. Blake, Duncan Blake."

She narrows her eyes a little before turning to a screen behind the bar.

"Great, I'm Darla. Come this way then, Mr Blake, and I'll show you to your room."

I follow her up a narrow staircase to a small room with leaded windows facing the village green. It's hardly the hotel suites I'm used to, but then, I don't know of another place for miles.

"The pub opens at three and we serve food from five, if you should need anything."

"Thanks." I'm tired, but it's probably jet lag and I could do with a rest. She leans against the doorframe with her arms crossed, regarding me.

"Are you here for the wedding?"

Oh, a nosy type then. Or maybe she's just trying to be polite. Still, I'm already nervous about why I'm here, so I don't want to talk about it.

"I can't see how it's any of your business." I am gruff, but to her credit, she doesn't bat an eyelid.

"This village is a bit off the beaten path. We don't get many visitors passing through, and yet every room is booked for the first time in I don't know how long. All of them are here for the wedding tomorrow."

"Assume I'm here for the same reason, then," I say, hoping to get rid of her so I can have a lie down.

"Hmm, I suppose you could be a journalist or a photographer. I just thought that with the name Blake, you could be family. And yet you're not staying at the house."

She's getting a bit too close to the truth for comfort. In fact, a lot too close.

"I said it was none of your business," I repeat, a bit sharper this time.

"I could make it my business. Are you here to cause trouble?"

What is this woman's problem? She continues before I can answer.

"Jackson and Luca are well liked in this town. We all wish them a happy day tomorrow. They both deserve it after all they've been through, so if you *are* here to cause trouble, you can leave now."

"No trouble, I promise." I hold my hands up in a gesture of supplication. She narrows her eyes again but seems satisfied, at least for now. She leaves and heads off downstairs. I'd heard through Isabel about the incident with David last year, and another guy who'd caused some grief. I'm pleased that Jackson has found a community to stick up for him, I'm just not comfortable being on the sharp end of it. My hope is for reconciliation, not to make things harder.

· · ·

I MANAGE to get some rest before heading to the bar for something to eat. It's busy, and I'm pleased just to sit and gather my thoughts.

"Penny for them?" Darla picks up the empty glass from my table.

"I don't know if I'm doing the right thing," I admit in a moment of weakness, cursing myself for not keeping my mouth shut.

"Tell me about it," she says, as she sits down on the vacant chair across from me.

I look round the pub, thinking she must have other patrons to tend to or, at the very least, better things to do. But I see the pub is largely empty now. I must've been sitting here, lost in my thoughts, for longer than I thought. So, against my better judgement, I tell her a very abridged version.

"I've known Jackson for nearly a year now, and for what it's worth, I think he'll be pleased to see you," she says, standing up to gather some more glasses.

I'm grateful for her words, as I'm already keyed up enough about tomorrow.

I MAKE sure I arrive a few minutes before the ceremony starts. Just enough time to get the lie of the land, but not enough to invite comment. The marquee is huge . . . this really *is* a big wedding. I'm grateful, as it'll make it easier to blend into the background. I don't want to make my presence known until after the ceremony. The colour scheme is pink and lilac, with silver accents, and it's all very elegant. There are a few people wandering around with cameras—press photographers, I assume. I hadn't realised how much of a celebrity Luca was, or how popular the gardens have become. This is like a society wedding. Still, it is to my advantage, because if it was a small wedding, where everyone knew everyone else, I'd stand out.

I see Darla in a group of people. She clocks me, and I see her smirk slightly, nod at me, and turn back to the group—that includes Jackson. I haven't seen my son in over twenty years, but I would know him anywhere. He's handsome, but more importantly, he also looks really happy. I'm so pleased for him. He doesn't look my way, so I assume Darla hasn't said anything to him. I make a mental note that she has gone up slightly in my estimation.

The group moves off, up through a meadow to a folly on the hill. I follow at a distance, appreciating the beautiful view, and I see why they thought this would be a good place for a wedding.

I remain at the back, keeping my eyes on Jackson, watching as he catches sight of his soon-to-be husband. My heart constricts a little as I see the love in his eyes. I'm both proud of him and pleased for him, but also sad that I've never had anyone special enough to look at that way. I also wasn't there for Jackson when he was younger, which adds to the feeling. I choke back a few tears as they say their vows, and I turn away before they finish and start making their way back to the marquee. I really need a drink—a stiff one—so I head to the bar.

Now comes the hard bit. A part of me wants to slink away, leave things as they are. I can see how happy he is. Maybe he won't want me in his life, serving as a reminder of his time before. But I've come from the other end of the Earth to see him and I would like to get to know the man my son has become. In the end, the decision is taken out of my hands. I feel a hand on my arm, and looking down, I see it's Darla. She gives me a little smile.

"I think there's someone you want to see?"

I look up, and Jackson is standing right in front of me. His eyes register shock first.

"Hello son," I sputter, almost losing the ability to speak.

"Dad?" His voice holds surprise, but also an element of hope. I feel tears welling up and I manage to speak round the lump in my throat.

"You looked fantastic up there."

I'm immediately pulled into an embrace and squeezed tightly. Over the years, I've run through many scenarios in my mind. This imagined meeting has had many outcomes, but none have had this one. Not this immediate hug and contact. I choke back tears full of regret that I hadn't got to know my son sooner.

Eventually, he releases me and pulls back.

"I'm sorry." It's inadequate, woefully inadequate. I can't make up for twenty years of absence.

He cracks a small, sad smile, and it breaks my heart. "You have a lot of explaining to do, but today is a happy day and I'm not letting anyone ruin it for me and Luca."

I'm not off the hook by a long way, but it's still much better than I deserve.

"I understand." Then, releasing the tension I was holding, I say, "Thank you."

He nods, then breaks out in a smile. "Would you like to meet Luca? He must be around here somewhere."

"Of course, I'd love to."

He scans around the marquee and then takes my arm and wends his way through some tables.

"Luca, baby," he whispers into the ear of his husband.

I'd seen Luca from afar during the ceremony, but as he turns around, I'm struck by his delicate features and gentian-coloured eyes. My son has very good taste.

"Luca, this is my dad."

He looks from me to Jackson and back, frowning. "I thought your dad left you."

"It's a long story, but maybe for another time," I cut in. "I'm pleased to meet you, Luca." I stick out my hand.

He takes it and smiles. "Okay, hello, err, Jackson's dad."

"It's Duncan."

"Then pleased to meet you, Duncan." His final word is drowned out by the sound of a glass smashing behind us.

CHAPTER 2

*H*arlen

I DON'T REGISTER that I've dropped the glass until I hear gasps and realise everyone is looking at me. I look at my feet, at the shards of glass and the liquid dripping from my shoes, and even then I can't do a thing about it. All my breath has gone and time stands still. In what feels like slow motion, I raise my head again and look straight into the eyes of the reason my hands could no longer function enough to keep hold of a drink. Eyes I haven't seen for thirty years.

Awareness of my surroundings floods back to me and I see people moving towards me, calling my name. I can't do this right now. I need to get out of here. I turn and stride out of the marquee and across to the carpark. Wrenching open the door of my Jeep, I climb in and slam the door. But I don't go anywhere. I put my arms on the steering wheel and rest my head on them, trying to draw air back into my lungs.

The last person I expected to see today is Duncan Blake.

Hell, I never expected to see him again—ever. Duncan Blake . . . Blake . . . Blake, oh fuck! Blake is a common enough name that I never thought there could be a connection. Why would I? But to see him standing next to Jackson, it was as clear as day. If this isn't fucking messed up already, Duncan fucking Blake is Jackson's fucking father. Apart from the incident last year with Jackson's prick of a brother, he hasn't mentioned his family at all. I'd assumed he had no contact with any of them.

I thump my hand onto the steering wheel in frustration. I have no clue what I'm going to do about this. Actually, yes, I do. I need a drink right *now*, since I'm wearing my last one. I start my Jeep and drive back to my cabin. My cabin. My sanctuary. The place where I've lived for the last twenty years. The only place where I've found some semblance of peace—never calmness, never happiness, barely contentment—but the place where I could at least live. But now? My whole world has tilted on its axis and this cabin no longer feels like my haven.

I head straight to the whisky and do the one thing I vowed I'd never do again. I blot out the world with drink.

CHAPTER 3

 uncan

I WATCH Harlen Davies march out of the marquee, as people rush towards him. There's a flurry of activity as the broken glass is swept away.

Luckily, no one is looking my way as I can't keep the surprise off my face. I can't believe I've just seen Harlen. I haven't seen him in . . . It must be thirty years. I feel a sharp pang somewhere around my solar plexus. We used to be good friends. When we were at college, I'd say we were best friends. But sadly, we grew apart when I got married to Gloria—she didn't approve of him—and I haven't seen him since. He saw me, though. Of that I'm sure. But I don't understand why he wouldn't have come over to say hello.

Someone returns and comes over to Jackson, shaking their head.

"I can't find him. His car's gone, too," he says.

"Okay, thanks. It's odd. Not like him at all," Jackson replies before turning back to me. I try to keep my features as neutral as possible.

"You're obviously very busy. I don't want to monopolise any more of your time on your special day," I say to him.

He looks at me, indecision etched across his face, so I try to make it easier for him.

"Jackson, if you'd allow it, I'd like to get to know you better." I let the sentence hang, so it will be completely up to him.

His expression settles into relief. "Yeah, I'd really like that. Why don't you come over tomorrow?"

"Tomorrow? You just got married. I'm sure you have other things to do."

Jackson laughs. "We have a house full of guests for the weekend. Nothing else is going to be happening."

"Are you sure? I've waited this long . . ."

"I'm sure. Anna is doing something for lunch, and I'll have plenty of time to have Luca to myself when we leave on Monday."

"Honeymoon?"

His eyes shine as he answers. "We're spending a week in Japan, to see the Sakura festival."

"That sounds lovely. I haven't seen it myself, but I've heard it's beautiful."

"I've been wanting to show it to Luca for ages. He's going to love it." He smiles at the thought, and I love that he finally has someone special in his life. I never met his ex-wife, but what I *have* heard makes my heart ache for what he went through. It was yet another part of his life I wasn't there for. I'm going to continue feeling guilty about this for a long time.

"So you'll come?" he asks.

"Yes. I'd love to." He nods, and I let him go so he can get back to his husband and all their friends. I also see some photographers heading his way for a photo shoot. I head back to the bar, in need of another drink.

I don't get to talk to Jackson again, but it's a good wedding and everyone seems to enjoy themselves. Jackson and Luca look great together—happy. Their first dance together looks well rehearsed, and fun too. I talk with a few of his friends, learning more about my son over the course of the evening than I have in the many years that have passed since I was a part of his life. I'm surprised that everyone seems so accommodating towards me, but I guess because Jackson is fine with my presence, no one else seems to have a problem. I dance with his friends, with Darla, and even with Luca. He said it's odd to meet his father-in-law on his wedding day, but he's pleased that Jackson will have a chance at a reconciliation. One he thought he'd never get. The shadow that crosses his face makes me think there's some darkness in his past. But it's not my business, and it's gone quickly enough, as though he's not letting it encroach on his special day.

As the evening winds down, I notice that Jackson and Luca are nowhere to be seen. I don't blame them for sneaking away early. I decide it's time for me to leave too, and head back to the pub.

It's only later, when I'm in bed, having left the curtains open so I can look out at the large moon hanging in the sky, that I allow myself to think about Harlen.

We were inseparable in college, even though he was studying arboriculture and I was studying architecture. He used to joke that we became friends because our courses were next to each other in the alphabet. It might be true, as I met him while we were standing in line to enrol for the student's union. For four years we hung out, did basically everything together, spoke about our families and our love lives. I miss the relationship I'd had with Harlen. I know it would likely be too much to recapture that friendship, but it might be good to catch up.

I'd liked his easy smile and humour, though the Harlen I'd glimpsed today didn't look like he smiled often anymore. His eyes held a haunted look, and I wondered idly if someone had caused it. He'd already suffered so much, and it would be sad if that's what had happened.

CHAPTER 4

$\mathcal{H}$arlen

I BLINK INTO THE GLOOM, waiting for my eyes to focus—except they don't. Instead, the pressure in my temple blossoms into throbbing, and my tongue feels like it's been left out in the desert for a week.

I try to move, and it kicks off several shades of agony throughout my body. I roll over and—

Hit the floor.

"Fuck!" I instinctively curl up, adding slightly winded to my growing list of complaints.

I push myself up to sitting, and then double over as the throbbing sledgehammers into my skull.

"Owww." I wedge the heels of my hands into my eye sockets, hoping it helps stop the dizziness.

It doesn't.

Being on the floor means I'm not in the bedroom. I've slept on the couch—in my clothes. In my suit. My best suit. Fuck!

The wedding. I ran out on Jackson and Luca. I need to apologise. Then I remember the reason for my crapulence, and a whole new world of hurt rains down on me.

The only clear thought I can manage is that drink is not the way. It never was the way, and why I avoided spirits most of the time. But I was in too much shock yesterday to remember that.

I stagger to my feet and stumble towards the kitchen, ricocheting off the coffee table and barking my shin.

"Fuck. I'm too old for this shit."

I grab a glass of water and take a painkiller. Before I can change my mind, I decide to pour away the rest of my whisky. I retrieve the bottle from under the coffee table, staring at the clear, empty bottle.

Shit. I drank it all. No wonder I feel like I've gone several rounds with a heavyweight champion with my hands tied behind my back.

I make it to the bathroom and add a sleeping tablet to the mix before heading to my bedroom. This time I manage to wriggle out of my clothes first—leaving them on the floor to deal with later—and crawl into bed, before glorious oblivion takes over.

When I wake, the sunlight streaming through the window warms my face. My head has settled into a dull hammering, which I can mostly ignore. Before I move, I take an inventory of the rest of my symptoms. Physically, I'm not in as bad a shape as I expected. But the fissure in my soul, the one I've spent thirty years trying to mend, feels like it's been ripped open with rusty barbed wire.

I drag myself to the edge of the bed, place my feet on the floor, and sit up. I wish I could feel numb, but I can't. Last night reminded me I cannot find the answer at the bottom of a bottle. But there's no easy fix; experience has taught me that. The only thing I can do is move from one moment to the next, focussing on the subsequent task. I have to narrow my world to the next physical thing. Make it take up all my attention. Leave no room for anything else. First on the list—a shower.

SHOWERED AND DRESSED, with a strong coffee in my hand, I feel better. No, not better, but I can cope for now. I've managed before and I can do it again. I head out to my workshop, to the only thing that has truly helped me. I select a new wood blank and load it onto the lathe. Losing myself in the feel and motion of creating something.

CHAPTER 5

uncan

WHEN I REACH Larchdown House the next morning, you would never know that there'd been a wedding the previous day. Everything has been cleared away—the marquee, bar, tables and chairs. Maybe the grass is a bit squashed from the false flooring that had been laid, but apart from that, you can't tell a thing.

The door is answered by a tall, very elegant, dark-haired woman. She also has a demeanour that looks like it takes no prisoners. I guess this must be the infamous Anna. I hadn't had a chance to meet her the previous day.

"Welcome. You must be the absent father." *Ouch*. She doesn't pull any punches.

"Anna, please don't frighten him away already. I don't need a bodyguard." Jackson appears behind her and she turns, conceding her place at the door with a shrug that shouts, "bullshit."

Jackson comes outside, shutting the door behind him.

"That's Anna. She is *very* protective of her friends, but when you get to know her, she's also very supportive."

He starts walking along the front of the house. "I thought we could talk in the garden first. The house is a bit busy and I could do with a break for now."

"I'm happy with that." I follow him, and he sets off towards the gardens. At first, he starts off with a spiel that sounds like it's been said hundreds of times. A true horticulturist's guide to the gardens. My chest swells with pride, listening to how passionate he is about the gardens and the flowers and the plans that they have to develop them further. It hits me, I have no right to feel that pride, and when he pauses for breath in what he describes as the rose garden, I stop him.

"Could we sit down for a minute?" I indicate a bench close by.

He sits, and I settle down beside him. For the first time since I saw him yesterday, he looks a little nervous, and I don't blame him as I am too.

"I'm sorry, Jackson. I'm sorry I haven't been there for you."

"I don't want your sorry, Dad." He stumbles over the title. "I want to know why? Why you left us? Why I cried myself to sleep for months after you went?" He stops and looks away, needing a moment.

A lump forms in my throat. I hadn't known that it had affected him so much. Not that it would have made a difference, it just would have made it a lot harder. But I didn't get a chance to explain back then.

I lean forward, resting my arms on my thighs. "What did your mother tell you happened?"

"I just want your side of the story, Dad."

I take a deep breath before answering. "Your mother and I had problems throughout our relationship. Perhaps we were too young, or perhaps we were just incompatible. We tried to make it work, but it became clear not long after you were born that we couldn't do it. We limped along for a few more years, but we started arguing, and finally agreed we didn't think it was a healthy environment for you all. At least we agreed on that much. So we separated, and I moved out. I still wanted to see you and support you. I came and took you out a few times, but I don't know if you remember that." He shakes his head like he doesn't recall those specific occasions, so I guess he was too young at the time.

"Your mother filed for divorce, and I had no reason to dispute it. I was pleased that she felt able to move on, hoping she'd find someone else." I pause for a minute, trying to decide how to say the next bit. I pause for so long that Jackson speaks.

"She never found someone else."

"I know. But I did—and that was the problem. I didn't meet another woman, I met a man. Peter. He was older than me and very kind. But your mother? She didn't like that. She had a real problem with the fact that her former husband was bisexual. I hadn't told her, as it was something I'd only discovered just before she fell pregnant with Isabel, so I didn't feel it was relevant. I didn't know it would cause so much of a problem."

Jackson lets out a bitter laugh but doesn't say anything, waiting for me to continue.

"I didn't know she was so opposed to it, that she'd take out a court order that prevented me from having any contact with you. I could pay maintenance, which I did—every penny—but I wasn't allowed to approach or contact you in any way."

Jackson turns and looks at me, hurt and confusion etched on his face. "I never knew this. That you were prevented from seeing us. I knew Mom had cut you off, but I was fed the line that you left because you'd found someone else and didn't want anything to do with us. I cried for so long, wanting you back, wishing that you wanted me too." He wipes a tear from his eyes, and I tentatively place an arm around his shoulder as he leans into me.

"I couldn't take that. Being in the same country and not being able to see you was too hard. I moved to Australia, which was as far away as possible. I set up my own architectural firm and I've been there ever since . . . Well, until a few days ago.

"When Isabel was eighteen, she found out where I was and contacted me. I sent her the airfare to come out and join me."

"I knew Isabel was in Australia, but I never knew you were there as well. I was never really that close to her." He sounds downcast, and I give his shoulder a squeeze.

"She regrets leaving you behind, but she believed you thought the same as your brother."

"I thought I did, too." He shrugs and lets out a sigh.

"She'd like to see you," I add. "And Luca."

He brightens. "Would she?"

"She would. And she has a husband, Gavin, and two children, Jane and Scott."

"I have a niece and nephew?" He shakes his head in wonder.

"They're great kids." I don't add that I'm trying to be the best grandad I can, trying to make up for not being there for my own children.

He's crying again, and I hug him.

"It's all a bit much. Having you here was shocking enough, but finding out I have more family to reconnect with and meet . . ."

"I know son. But I'm so happy you've allowed me the chance to talk, and didn't kick me out."

"I am *not* my brother."

"Yeah, Darla said as much."

"You told Darla?" He draws back, with a smirk shining through his damp cheeks. "No, don't answer that. I know Darla."

"Well, she did help me when I was having second thoughts about being here."

"She's a good friend, even if she is rather too good at getting people to talk."

He stands up, and I follow. We continue through the garden, heading back towards the house. We walk in silence for a while, but then he speaks.

"I can't change our plans this week, but maybe in the autumn, after we close the gardens, Luca and I could visit Isabel."

"I think she would like that."

"What about you, Dad? What are your plans?"

"I haven't got any at the moment. My company is in good hands. Gavin—I think you'll like him—works for me, and is well able to look after things. I was waiting to see how things were when I met you."

"Well, I'd love it if you could stay long enough that I can see more of you when we get back."

"I can stay for a while. I'd really like that."

He hugs me, giving me a squeeze. "Thanks Dad." Then he releases me. "Now, can I offer you a coffee? Tea? Will you stay for lunch?"

CHAPTER 6

 arlen

I CONTINUE CREATING, unable to stop. I remember to grab a few brief snatches of sleep sometime in the night, but they don't last long. I'm fuelled by passion and coffee. Like a madman, I carve and gouge the wood, working by feel, modifying and refining it as the grain of the wood demands. It's organic, and you have to be sympathetic to its needs. I coax the shape I have in my head out of it. Eventually, after I don't know how long but at least twenty-four hours, I put down my tools and stand back.

Even I know it's good. It might be some of my best work. I also know it will never be seen by anyone else. This piece is for me only. It's a carved heart, captured wholly within an intricate cage. All made from one piece of wood.

I'm spent, drained, and feeling more like myself. I think I can get through this as long as I stay up here, out of the way.

Surely Duncan can't be around forever. I know he's just found his son again, but surely he has a life somewhere else, a partner even. Maybe a whole new family. No, I can't think like that. The thought that he might have someone prompts a wave of nausea and almost undoes all the time I've spent carving. Back to focussing on one task at a time. I blow out a breath and move the piece to a shelf out of the way, then set to cleaning up the workshop. After putting all the tools back into their holders and gathering the wood shavings, I'm sweeping up when I hear a car pull up outside.

I imagine it's someone checking up on me. I did disappear on Saturday, after all. Was it only forty-eight hours ago? Though no one came by yesterday—or maybe they did and I didn't notice them. I step out to greet whoever drew the short straw. They at least don't need to see me moping around in self-pity.

I think it might be Johan. We've become quite good friends, and I've yet to see him since he returned from Sweden. I was surprised to hear that he and Cole had got married, but I'm also pleased, as they're perfect together and they both deserve happiness. But it's not Johan. I don't recognise the vehicle that pulls up beside my Jeep.

My stomach twists when I see who it is. *Duncan.* Why is the universe doing this to me?

I consider hiding back inside my workshop and waiting until he's gone, but he's already seen me.

I try to stop the shaking that's started. I'll be polite, get rid of him as soon as possible, and hopefully he'll leave me alone.

"Hi Harlen," he says as soon as he gets out of the car, his face flashing a smile of perfect white teeth. "I thought it was you that I saw on Saturday."

His teeth aren't the only perfect thing. He looks *hot*. In my memory, he's always twenty-one, as that's how old we both

25

were the last time I saw him. But at fifty, damn, he's aged well. He's fit and toned, and his skin is tanned and oh-so perfect. I mean, I'm also fit from scaling trees, but I live in England— white and pasty is our national colour. I'm also aware I haven't shaved since before the wedding, though my record on bothering to do that can be considered haphazard at best.

He doesn't hide the grey in his hair—just a bit at the temples—which makes him look distinguished, whereas I just look grizzled. My straggly, greying hair is just a bit too long, so it falls in my face but is not long enough to tie back. And with a few days of scruff, I must look like an old man of the woods, which is basically true. It doesn't help that I'm covered in dust from the workshop. I need a shower, whilst he looks like he's just stepped out of a men's fashion magazine. It all serves to make me hate him a little bit more. I swallow it all, though.

"Duncan, this is a surprise." There's no way I'm owning up to seeing him on Saturday. I don't want him knowing what effect he has on me. "What are you doing in Larchdown?"

"Visiting my son. Attending his wedding." The smooth bastard. I'll take him down a peg.

"Jackson's a good friend of mine," I grind out, hoping he takes the hint that I know he hasn't just dropped in as if he hasn't been absent for years.

"How do you know . . ."

"He looks like you, and anyway, Luca's father is dead." I watch as a dark frown flits across his face, filing away the information that he didn't know. I wait, to see what he'll say next—what he's actually here for.

"I thought we could catch up." I suppress a sharp laugh. *Catch up!*

"Duncan, it's been thirty years."

He gives a disarming shrug and a smile. "Well, let's not make it any longer."

He's not going to go away. I scrub my hand down my face. No, he still hasn't disappeared. I sigh.

"Do you want a coffee, tea, or whatever you drink down under?"

I don't wait for him to answer, instead turning towards the cabin. He can come in or not, I don't care.

I enter and head to the kitchen area, filling the kettle. I know the exact moment he enters the cabin as I hear him exclaim. While my back is turned, I allow myself a small smile, glad I could surprise him. He may be the architect, but I'm not without skills and I know my home is impressive. I know he'll be taking in the space, and how it's built with the organic nature of the wood in mind. How it almost flows round the forest.

I make sure my face is a straight mask before I turn back round.

"What will it be? Tea or Coffee?" But he's standing wide-eyed, gazing around and appreciating that even though it's made completely of wood, it is light and airy, and looks a lot bigger than it is.

"This is amazing." He gives me a grin. The first genuine expression I've seen on him, and it takes my breath away. He's still gorgeous.

"I built it." My clipped voice does nothing to diminish his brilliance.

"That's incredible. I've worked with steel and concrete for so long that I've forgotten how beautiful natural materials can be." He heads over to the counter that separates the kitchen from the rest of the space, but he's still looking round him. "Coffee would be great, thanks."

I load in a pod and flip the machine on. While it makes its usual noises, I fetch a couple of mugs and grab the milk from the fridge—anything to keep myself busy. Anything other than that, I am not allowing myself to think.

I place a mug of black coffee in front of him, with sugar and milk within reach. He can sort himself out. I ignore the part of me that notices he takes it the same way he's always done. I pick up my own cup and head over to the living area, sitting on a chair. I gesture to the couch, and he sits. Again I wait for him, to see how he wants to play this.

"What have you been up to?" he asks, stretching his legs out and seeming to be annoyingly at ease.

"I'm a tree surgeon. I've been here twenty years, that's it."

He looks round the room, as if he's looking for evidence of another person. If he is, he won't find it. I haven't been with anyone for a few years.

No one was right. No one was *him*.

"You?" I'm finding it hard to speak, and that's all I can manage while staying polite.

"I separated from Gloria and now I live in Sydney. I have my own architectural firm there. I'm close to my daughter and her partner, and my grandchildren."

It sounds so perfect, that his words have buried themselves in my heart and thrown away the key. I've had enough of trying. I'm jittery and I don't like how he can make me feel like this.

"So the whole family thing worked out for you then?" It's a very low shot and I know it, but I want to hurt him. I want to make him feel a little bit of what I've felt for so long. It gives me a small sense of satisfaction that it hits home. I'm angry and hurt that the reason I gave him up never worked out, that my sacrifice was for nothing. My victory is short-lived, as his face falls and he looks hurt. I don't like that look on him.

He stands up. "This was a mistake. You've changed Harlen."

It was. And he was damn right I'd changed. Thirty years of heartache can do that to a person.

"I should go."

Yeah, you should.

I stand as well, following him to the door. When he gets there, he turns and suddenly I'm too close. I catch a whiff of his scent, and while he might use different products now, beneath them he still smells the same as he did all those years ago. Something shifts in my memory and I can't think of now, only of back then, and I take the same action. Without thinking, he's up against the wall, and my lips have claimed him. And it feels like . . .

Home.

And everything I remember and have dreamed of every day for thirty years.

I almost groan at how perfect he feels. How I've waited for a return to those lips which are shaped to fit my own.

It reminds me of unsaid promises waiting to be whispered against each other's skin.

I want more of it . . .

I love it . . .

And . . .

And . . .

I hate it.

I hate myself. I hate him. I hate the day I let him go and the day he walked back into my life. I hate that I'm not the same person anymore. I'm too broken to deserve this. I hate that he isn't resisting me, that it could be this easy. I break from kissing him and push myself back. His mouth is slightly parted as he tries to recover his breath. His lips are bruised, wet, and glistening. He's still gorgeous, and I clamp down a hold on my heart. I can't do this. The last time this happened, his next move was to kiss me back, and I will not let that happen.

"You should go." I sound gruff, but I'm barely holding it together. He slowly blinks his eyes as if coming out of a daze. Confusion takes over as he realises what has happened.

"I—" he starts, but I don't want him to speak. If he does, I might break my resolve.

"Just go, Duncan." I turn away so he doesn't see the tears falling down my face. I head to my bedroom and slam the door behind me, leaving him to find his own way out. I know I'm being a dick, but I'm past caring. Nothing feels right anymore and I want it to stop.

CHAPTER 7

 uncan

I STARE after Harlen as he storms up the stairs and slams a door behind him. My brain is scrambled. I have no idea what just happened. Well, I do, but I don't know why.

Harlen had acted prickly since I got here, but then he kissed me. A small part of my subconscious registers that I let him. I could've said no, I could've pushed him off. But I did neither of those things.

That he doesn't want me here though is plain enough and I push off from the wall where I'm leaning and leave. I drive back to the village, my stomach flipping, and my chest tight in a confusion of feelings.

I MAKE A FEW CALLS, catching up with a few questions Gavin has about business, and have a video call with Isabel and the kids. Due to the time difference, it's late before I get to bed, but sleep eludes me and I find my thoughts turning back to Harlen. I'm disappointed that he clearly doesn't want to be friends again. Admittedly, we haven't spoken for thirty years and can't just pick it up again, but he doesn't even seem to want to try. He's acting like he hates me. Except for the kiss which, if I'm being honest with myself, I liked.

My cock twitches at the memory of those brief moments and I groan. I'm sure it's only because it's been so long since I've kissed anyone. A kiss from anything with a heartbeat would probably have had the same effect, and I refuse to believe otherwise.

Harlen and I used to be so close, and I'd thought of him almost as a brother. We could talk about anything.

It was to Harlen that I'd confided I thought I might be bi, in our final year, about a month before our final exams.

I remember the kiss we shared when I told him. Or rather, *he'd* kissed *me*. I even recall what he'd said . . .

"How do you know you're bi if you've never kissed a guy?" he asked, *eyes full of mischief.*

He had me pressed up against the wall and was kissing me before I'd managed more than a stammered, "I just do." His tongue exploring as I let him, his mouth taking my breath as I sucked him in, he broke the kiss just before I passed out from lack of oxygen.

He stood back, raising his eyebrow with a cocky, "well?" and a grin plastered on his face. It was I who initiated the second kiss, wanting to taste him, wanting to feel the warmth that was spreading throughout my body. Desperate to explore the fluttering in my chest that being near him suddenly evoked.

But then guilt had risen through me as my brain took over and I belatedly remembered I was still seeing Gloria. I broke off the kiss.

"Gloria," I muttered, as I severed the contact with him.

"You kiss me and the name on your lips is your girlfriend?"

Harlen had looked angry, and I didn't blame him. It wasn't a smart move, but I needed to remind myself that it wasn't right.

"Yeah, sorry. I shouldn't have done that."

"Kissed me or said her name?" He didn't look like he accepted my apology. He wanted an explanation.

"Both." His face looked crestfallen, and my guilt notched up a little.

I THINK that night damaged my friendship with my best friend. We seemed to grow apart after that. It was a tough time. We both had our final exams, and Gloria found out she was pregnant.

A family was something I'd dreamed of having, eventually. Maybe not straight out of college, but I guess the universe had other ideas. Not that it worked out well for me in that respect. It hadn't been the wonderful experience I'd hoped for; only having contact with one of my three children. Though with Jackson, hopefully I can make it two. I don't think I can ever reconcile with David. He'll never accept my lifestyle, and while that's up to him, it saddens me he thinks like that.

I'm looking forward to seeing Jackson again, getting to know him better when he and Luca return from their honeymoon, and it's with these thoughts that I finally drift off to sleep.

I SPEND the next few days driving round the area, familiarising myself with the layout of the land and looking for potential sites. Now that I've reconnected with Jackson, and the first meeting went very well, I feel hopeful about the future. If he accepts me back into his life, I'd like to stay awhile. I like the idea of opening a UK office for my company, leaving Gavin in charge of the Australian office. I might even build a house. I've had some design ideas in my head for a while, but it's only being in the English landscape that they've come together, and I think they might actually work. It's early days yet, but having a look around doesn't hurt and gives me something to do for the week.

It's Friday night and I've been in England, in Larchdown, for just over a week. I'm enjoying a pint of beer from a local brewery, a treat I don't usually have in Australia. I have a book and although it is open, it's not really grabbing my attention.

A hulking shape looms in my peripheral vision and I see a pair of sturdy forearms rest on the bar next to me. I have to look up into his face as he's so tall, and when I do, I'm staring into some piercing blue eyes, framed by ginger whiskers and an impressive beard. The eyes crinkle and I receive a wide smile.

This must be Keith. I'd seen him at the wedding, but we hadn't really been introduced.

"It's no fun to be on your own on a Friday night."

"I've nothing else to do."

"You're welcome to join us. We usually get together on a Friday night to relax and catch up on village gossip."

"Oh, am I village gossip?"

He guffawed loudly, his head thrown back in glee.

"Well, the way I see it, you could either *be* the gossip, or you can join in the gossip."

"So if I don't come and join you, then you'll talk about me?"

"We might do." He gives an unassuming shrug, but his eyes hold a twinkle, and I look past him to where he indicated, seeing a group of people.

"Or we might just want information straight from the horse's mouth, so to speak." He chuckles.

I'm not sure. I don't know these people very well. He must've seen my indecision as he leans a little closer.

"We don't bite." I have to laugh. Standing, I signal with my hand for him to lead the way. He introduces the group: himself, his husband Ben, Ben's half-brother Johan, and Johan's husband Cole. Also at the table are Cole's brother Tom, and Tom's wife Megan, as well as Paul and Sally. He explains that the group fluctuates depending on who's available at the time, and usually Jackson and Luca join them.

I notice, with equal parts relief and disappointment, that Harlen isn't part of the group. I don't know if he joins them or not. Keith pulls up another chair.

"Sit yerself down." I obey.

"So, Jackson's dad, do you have a name?"

I groan a little. "So you *have* been gossiping," I say in mock horror.

"Believe me, the only thing more exciting than the fanciest wedding we've seen in a long time, is the sudden appearance of a long-lost relative at that wedding."

I have to concede to him that point.

"It's Duncan."

"Well Duncan, where have you been hiding yerself for however long?"

I'm going to get the full interrogation then.

"I've been in Australia for twenty years. I'm an architect. I have my own company there."

I decide to give them a few more details, but I also want to set some boundaries.

"But I will not be telling you anything about my relationship with Jackson. I've only just reconnected with him and it's early days. If he wants to tell you anything later, then that's up to him, but you won't get it from me."

There's a slight pause after I deliver my speech, then Keith lets out another laugh and claps one of his huge hands on my shoulder.

"You'll do for us."

I feel like I've passed some sort of test. He gives me a wink, and I get the feeling he is the group's unofficial leader, and also possibly the biggest gossip in the village.

"So if you can't talk about Jackson, tell us about yourself. Do you have a significant other waiting for you back in Oz?"

"No, there's no one. I'm currently single." I don't add, that apart from the strange kiss with Harlen at the beginning of the week, I haven't even kissed anyone in a long time, let alone done anything else.

I have spent some time over the last few days thinking about that kiss, but I'm no closer to understanding what went on. I haven't been up to the cabin again. I wasn't sure what welcome I'd get, and if Harlan didn't want to be friends, then so be it, but it was not without some sadness that I let it go.

I don't realise that I've drifted into my own thoughts until I feel a bump against me and I realise I've been asked a question

"How long are you staying?"

I try to recover my thoughts quickly. "I don't know. I haven't really planned as far as that, but a couple more weeks at least."

I'm not going to tell them about some of my hopes and plans, as that's largely down to Jackson. I catch a look between Keith and his husband, Ben. Ben gives him a little eye roll.

"So you'll be around to help on Monday, then?" Keith asks.

"Monday?"

"Don't let him press-gang you into anything you don't want to do," Ben says. But I'm intrigued.

"Why, what's Monday?"

"The May Day village fete." Keith answers. "We always need more pairs of hands if you feel like helping."

Being out of the country for so long, I'd forgotten about May Day celebrations and village fetes. How quaint that sounds. I'm definitely interested in helping.

"I'd love to help out if I can." Keith looks pleased and Ben shakes his head at him, but with a smile on his face, so I assume that's an old debate for them. I seem to no longer be a source of interest for the group as the conversation turns away to other subjects, and I just take a passive role and let it wash over me. When I finish my drink, I offer to buy the group a round, which meets with their approval. It all seems very companionable until Darla calls last orders a few hours later. I stand up and stretch, suddenly very tired. I'm not sure what the next few days will hold. Though Jackson will be returning from his honeymoon and has invited me up to the house again.

CHAPTER 8

 uncan

I WAKE EARLY, watching the light dapple across the room as the sun slowly rises. I allow my thoughts to drift back to yesterday, and seeing Jackson again after his return from his honeymoon. He looked happy and I'm pleased that he's found someone who loves him. He adores Luca, and it's a delight to see them together. I tried to apologise again for the past, but he wouldn't let me.

He rationalised, that everything that'd happened, had led him along the path that eventually brought him to Larchdown —and to Luca. That every hardship he endured was worth it. He's wise beyond his years, and I marvel how he can think that way, as it certainly wasn't my influence.

I'm happy that he wants me in his life, and we discussed the plans I have to be a more permanent fixture in his life. Plans I will put into place with a visit to the land agency tomorrow.

Today, however, I've agreed to help at the village fete.

Checking my watch, I realise I need to get a move on. I'm planning to meet Jackson in half an hour. Even though he's been away for a week and is getting ready to open the gardens to the public soon, he's still making time to help at the fete. He said it holds a special place in his heart, and he loves to give back to a community who welcomed him with open arms when he had no one. I admit I find the people of Larchdown an accommodating group, and I too have been made to feel welcome. Well, except for one person; the one who I thought might have been the opposite. I push back the covers and get up. I'm *not* thinking about Harlen at the moment. But if I'm honest, deep down, I'm longing to see him again.

I MEET Jackson and Keith on the village green, Keith proudly strutting around in a kilt and looking damn fine doing it, too. I'm soon put to work for several hours helping set up the marquee and the booths for the retailers. I discover that there are many varied and eclectic craft groups and artists in Larchdown, and I'm happy to help them carry their items to their booths and help set up tables and display cases. By the time the fete opens at ten, I'm ready for a break. I grab a bottle of water and find a space in the shade to rest. I think I must have drifted off as I become aware of someone flopping down next to me.

"No slacking on the job."

I open an eye and see Keith grinning at me.

I let out a groan. "It's alright for you young ones. Old folks like me need a rest." I don't add that these days my life consists mostly of sitting in front of a computer, not doing physical work. I keep myself in reasonable shape by doing yoga, but it's no replacement for good cardio exercise.

"Nonsense, I just don't think you're used to it. Don't worry, I'm sure that someone in Larchdown will find something for you to do."

"Urgh, thanks. Now leave me alone to sleep."

"Come on, the pub is open now. Let me buy you a drink."

"Isn't it a bit early?"

"It's a bank holiday in England, I don't think there is a too early." He rises and offers me a hand up, which I accept. "Where have you been? The other side of the world?" He laughs at his own joke, and I follow him across to The Blacksmith's Arms. A flashback to my university days pushes its way into my head, and I remember several Sundays spent relaxing in the sun with a pint—with Harlen. I find myself looking round for him, and think I see him across the village green before Keith pulls me into the pub for a drink.

Keith is good company, but after one drink his presence is required elsewhere. I need something to eat, so I head back and wander through the fete, looking at the food stalls, trying to decide what to sample first.

Having decided on a crêpe filled with ham and cheese, I walk amongst the craft stalls. My eye is drawn to some intricate carvings, and I'm in the booth before I realise it reminds me of some of the pieces I saw at Harlen's cabin. I spin round and see him watching me, a wary look on his face. I try to ignore the squeezing feeling starting in my chest.

The silence stretches between us and becomes uncomfortable. I glance round again, trying to decide if I ought to bring up what happened the other day. I lose my nerve.

"These are beautiful." I gesture to the work he has for sale. Beautiful isn't an adequate description; he's really skilled.

"Everyone's got to have a hobby." He shrugs. His face is like stone, giving nothing away.

I summon some courage. "Harlen—" But then a young couple come into his booth. He turns away to answer their question, and the moment has gone. I give him another glance, but he's not looking my way. I sigh and turn away. Maybe this wasn't the right place to try talking with him. I hope I'll get a chance soon. I'm going to be around for a while and there's this feeling I get when he's close, like charged energy. It needs to be addressed. I don't go back to his stall during the rest of the fete. I help take down the marquee at the end of the day. I look for Harlen, but his booth is empty. He's packed up and gone.

CHAPTER 9

*H*arlen

I USUALLY ENJOY the May Day fete in the village. It's grown over the years and is a real community event. It's also one of the few places where I showcase my work. Whilst I'm a tree surgeon by trade, the carving and woodturning is my hobby, my way of creating a bit of beauty out of the materials around me. It's also been the one thing that's kept me sane and sober for years.

But this year I'm on edge and I know why. This year *he* will be here. I've avoided the village for most of the week. Knowing he'll be around somewhere. Darla came and visited me on Monday, worried about my hasty departure from the wedding. But what could I tell her? I feigned feeling ill, but assured her it wasn't to do with the catering at the event. That I'd eaten something off the night before and hadn't felt well. I doubt she bought it, but I wasn't going to tell her the truth.

Why did I have to suffer a moment of weakness and kiss him? All I've wanted to do since then is repeat it . . . and do a whole lot more. It's been on my mind pretty much constantly, and that he can have this effect on me still, even after all these years, makes me hate him for it.

I watch him as he helps out at the fete. Of course Keith, in charge of organising volunteers, would have roped him in. No one can resist Keith if he thinks you can do something to help. I steal glances while I'm setting up my stall. I watch him take a breather and wipe sweat from his brow. I can't avert my eyes and I wonder what it tastes like, how I'd like to have his sweaty body in my arms. I turn away, despising myself and hating that he can make me feel like this, especially after what happened. And he comes along and acts like he has no idea of what he does to me. Like he has no clue of the scars he left on my soul.

I put him out of my mind. Surely he must be going back to whatever cave he crawled out of soon enough, and I won't have to look at his handsome face anymore.

I'm lost in my thoughts, having managed to focus on something other than Duncan Blake for once, only for him to appear at my stall. I prop myself up on my table and cross my arms, staring at him. I know he wants to say something about what happened, ask why I kissed him. But he looks uncomfortable, and I derive some sort of pleasure from watching him squirm. Eventually he comments on the work, and I shrug. I don't really know what else to say. I hadn't wanted to answer him at all, but that fucking tanned, beautiful face made me do it. I wait for him to make the next move, ask the next question, to see if he'll finally say something. Then some customers come into the booth, and I pointedly ignore him and tend to their needs.

When I next glance up he's gone, but the pressure I feel in my chest hasn't. As soon as the crowds start to thin and the event winds down, I pack my stuff up and leave. The only option is for me to put distance between us.

CHAPTER 10

 uncan

I STAND on the site and look around me. It's perfect. The thick woods border one edge. The side of the valley slopes gently and there are larger trees dotted about. At the bottom is a river. The meadow to the other side looks over the downs and the views are stunning. I can imagine waking up to that every morning. I can't wait to make it a reality. I know I have to wait for the surveys to come through, but it is virgin land, so there shouldn't be a problem there.

Planning permission might be more tricky, but it isn't a protected area, and with the design I have in mind it won't be intrusive. It'll be a green build, utilising the latest technology. I'm also planning to offer it—occasionally—as a holiday let, for those times when I have to go back to Australia. So there's a tourism element that I hope will sway the planners. The survey should take a couple of weeks to get back, then I can sign on the dotted line and make this little corner of the valley mine.

Planning could take a few months, so I need to get started on the designs as soon as possible.

I spend a few more minutes just taking in the fresh, clean air. It's a far cry from the centre of Sydney, and while I've got used to the hustle and bustle of city life, I can appreciate the serenity of the forest, even welcome it.

Whether it's the influence of the forest or because my thoughts are never far from him at the moment, my mind wanders to Harlen again. Since the kiss, small memories keep surfacing—remembrances of touches, of looks he used to give me—and I feel a sense of unease, as if something isn't quite right. I can't put my finger on it. But what I *do* know is, even though he's quite adamant that he doesn't want me around and can barely stand the sight of me, I have a yearning to feel his lips again. I'm also starting to remember feelings I never allowed myself to explore back then. I didn't recognise them at the time, only experience and hindsight have given them a new perspective. Every time I think of his mournful eyes, I find myself wanting to lift the sadness that hangs over him, and I want a whole lot more than just his lips.

CHAPTER 11

$\mathcal{H}$arlen

I'VE AVOIDED Larchdown House since the wedding, but I know that Jackson and Luca are getting ready to open it to the public in a few weeks, and I need to check on some trees first. There had been some damage to some of the older trees during the winter storms, so I need to assess them and see what can be saved, or what needs to be taken down to make it safe.

As I pull my Jeep up in the circular driveway at the front of the house, Jackson comes out to greet me.

He offers me a coffee before we get started, and as I usually accept, I think it would be considered odd if I didn't.

"I'm really sorry about disappearing on you like that," I offer as a conversation starter when he hands me a mug of coffee.

He frowns. "Are you okay? Darla said that you weren't well."

"I'm fine now, thanks. It was just something I ate—the night before, that is. I thought I was alright, but it just seemed to hit me then."

"As long as you're alright, that's the main thing." He smiles his concern at me and I feel bad for lying, but there's no chance I'm going to tell him the truth. After all, he's just reunited with his father. I was curious if Duncan had said anything, though.

"So, that must have been a surprise, your dad turning up out of the blue."

"Yeah." His face changes to one of delight, and I feel a stab of jealousy that he's so happy. God, I feel evil that something that makes him so happy evokes that emotion in me. I clamp down the thoughts and listen to him as he tells me, that whilst he'd spent so long thinking his father had wanted nothing to do with him, he'd held a small grain of hope that one day he would see him again. That he turned up on his wedding day was, to Jackson, the icing on the cake of a perfect day.

As much as having Duncan in Larchdown is ripping me apart, I can't help but be pleased that Jackson is so happy. He deserves to be. But his next revelation chills me to the bone.

"I'm pleased that he's planning to stay around for a while, too."

"Doesn't he have a business back in Australia? Or wherever he comes from?" I quickly add on the end, not wanting to let on that I know that much about him.

"Not for a while. He says that Gavin, that's my sister's husband, so I guess my brother-in-law..." He pauses for a moment as if he's realising that fact for the first time, and he smiles, pleased with the thought. "Anyway, he can look after things there for a while. Dad wants to start a branch of the company here, in England."

"That'll be nice for you." I grit my teeth as I say it, not trusting myself to say anything further. I draw a breath to compose myself, and turn his attention back to the work I need to do. "I'm sure you're very busy right now. Why don't you show me these trees that need looking at?"

If Jackson notices anything odd in my manner, he doesn't

47

say anything, and soon we're walking through the garden and towards the avenue of trees that borders one of the main paths. The damage isn't too bad, but it will take a couple of days' work to sort them out, so I arrange to start the following day. As I'm leaving, Jackson stops me by my Jeep.

"We're having a barbecue on Sunday evening, after opening weekend, for friends and all those who've helped us. You will come, won't you?"

I hesitate. Normally, I would have said yes without question. Jackson frowns.

"Please come. We'd like it very much."

I find myself agreeing, even though I'm not sure it's a good idea, as no doubt Duncan will be there. I sigh. If he's going to be around for a while, then I can't avoid him forever. Perhaps it'll be safer to meet in the company of others. I'm not sure what I would do if we were alone.

CHAPTER 12

uncan

"Is it odd, seeing strangers in your garden?" I ask Jackson, as we watch the public milling about and enjoying the space. It's Sunday and there are even more visitors than there were yesterday. From our vantage point at the folly, we can pretty much see over the whole of the gardens. Maybe not quite as far as the orchard, but still a good view.

"Sometimes," he laughs. "But we're only open weekends, so we get a lot of time when there's no one about and it helps us appreciate it more. And I can't complain, as it brings in enough money to keep the gardens and the house going. So, I don't have to work elsewhere, and Luca can concentrate on his art."

"I'd like to see some of his work." I've heard he's very talented. "I'm thinking of having some for the new house."

Jackson breaks out into a wide smile. "You've got the land then."

I hold up my hand. "Not quite. I'm still waiting for the land survey, which is supposed to come through this week, but there shouldn't be any problems." Jackson pulls me into a hug. I relish it, not having had the chance to hug him as a kid.

"That's great, Dad. I'm looking forward to having you close."

He releases me, glancing around quickly. "Look, as we start closing up, I want to check that everything's alright. Are you still happy to help with the barbecue?"

"Son, I've lived in Australia for twenty years. I think I know my way around a barbecue."

He laughs. "Really?"

No, not really. I live in a penthouse suite in an apartment block I designed, not the bush. But I have attended plenty of them, especially with Gavin and Isabel, who live in the suburbs. But he finds it amusing and is still chuckling as he heads down the slope to the rest of the gardens. I turn and look out at the view across the downs from the folly, stopping for a few moments to rest on a stone bench.

I SPEND the next hour helping Luca. There's a large flagged area outside of the kitchen. I suppose you would call it a patio, but it isn't formal; it's old and in keeping with the house. It's hedged, to mark the boundary between the public gardens and the private areas close to the house itself. Luca puts me to work setting out tables and chairs. The gathering will be fairly small, just friends and a few of the staff from the gardens. There are Ethel and Dorothy, who look after the entries and the small gift shop, and Alex, who took over running the catering cabin, branching out from helping his dad, the chef at The Blacksmith's Arms.

The furniture is new and Luca fusses over where it should go, so I find myself moving it a couple of times before he's happy. Whilst he tells me they have hosted a few parties before, this is the first since their wedding, and he looks flustered. I don't know him well, and I would like to change that, but right now he looks like he's going to break.

"Hey, breathe," I say, as I watch him crumple into a chair, hunching over himself.

I sit down next to him, checking if he's okay, but unable to do much. After a few minutes, he raises his head and gives me a weak smile.

"You'd have thought I'd be used to these by now."

"Parties or panic attacks?"

He lets out a small laugh. "Both."

"It's just a few friends, so what are you worried about?"

He gives a little sigh. "Up till now, every party we've had has been Anna's doing. I've let her organise everything. This is the first time I've had to go it alone. I want to make Jackson proud of me."

"Oh, I think Jackson's already proud of you. He adores you."

His elfin features brighten at that, and then he frowns and looks down.

"And I wanted to impress you."

"Me?"

"You *are* my father-in-law."

"Luca, listen to me." I wait until he's looking at me. "I haven't exactly been the best father to Jackson. Some of it wasn't my fault, but some of it *was*, and I could have reached out sooner. I'm not proud of that. I've only been back in his life for five minutes. I'm not someone you need to impress. I'm happy that he's found someone to make him happy. That's all I've ever wanted for him. And you do make him happy, Luca. I'm the one who should be trying to impress you. To see if I'm worthy of being your father-in-law."

He takes a deep breath and straightens up, no longer looking so worried.

"Thank you. That's helped me a lot."

I stand and hold out my hand to help him up. He takes it and rises.

"Can I hug you?" He sounds so tentative that my heart melts a little at his sweetness and I can see how Jackson fell for him.

"Of course." He wraps his arms around me, and I hug him back.

"P—Please can I call you Dad?"

That stuns me for a minute and I let out a little laugh, as it seems so incredible. But I realise he's serious and remember he's never really had a father.

"If you want, then I'm okay with that."

He visibly relaxes against me as if he'd been expecting me to refuse, and I hug him a little tighter.

Eventually, I pull back and look at him. "Will Jackson be alright with you calling me Dad?"

He gives me a flash of a mischievous grin. "He said I had to ask you myself."

I shake my head in amusement, but inside my heart is full that they discussed me and want me in their lives enough for this. I came from Australia not knowing if my son would even want to know me and now, not only has he welcomed me with open arms, I've gained another son as well.

My good mood continues, as I help Luca set up for the barbecue and help prep some of the food. He tells me about some of his artwork, and from what I hear, I'm keen to see it. I tell him about my plans for the house and how I'd like to have a few pieces to hang in the space.

Jackson appears as I'm in the kitchen chopping vegetables for a salad and Luca is setting out some of the drinks for the guests. I glance over as he comes in through the door, and catch a silent exchange between him and Luca. I see Luca nod and then Jackson heads over to me. He places a hand on my shoulder and gives it a squeeze, whispering a "thank you," as he passes. I feel like I've somehow passed a test, but I'm pleased. I look back over at Luca, and he's smiling shyly at me.

I realise that I want what they have—not that I ever could. No one could be as cute as they are, and I don't really want cute. I prefer things a bit . . . rougher. What I want is someone to understand me so well that words aren't necessary. Someone to look out for me, and for me to look out for them. Someone who understands me on a soul-deep level. I grit my teeth a little, as at fifty, that's unlikely to happen. But hey, a guy can dream.

I take some of the dishes outside, not realising that guests have started arriving. The usual gang from Friday nights in the pub are here, as well as Dorothy and Ethel, who are sitting on a couple of chairs, giggling like schoolgirls despite their advanced age. Alex is talking to Ben, Cole is standing near the drinks table talking to Paul and Megan, while Keith, Jackson, and Johan are having a discussion about how best to manage the barbecue—which makes me laugh, because it is so stereo-typically male. What is it about cooking food outdoors that does that? I can almost smell the testosterone from where I'm placing the dishes on the table. I head back to the kitchen to help Luca bring out the last few things. When I come out, Jackson and Johan are still staring at the grill, but Keith has moved, and I track to where he's standing with Harlen, who has just arrived.

My stomach flips and I've just lost my appetite. I suppose it's natural that he'd be here, and I want to see him. But this is far too public. I feel much too exposed. He looks my way and his face goes stony, but his eyes burn with an intensity that warms me to the core.

The more he glowers, the more I find my insides catching fire, until I have to look away, turn away, before he and everyone else notices the effect he's having on me.

As I turn my back on him, I can still feel his gaze burning into me and I take a breath to steady myself.

I distract myself by talking to Luca, standing next to Jackson, and eventually my stomach settles so I can enjoy the moment. In truth, it's everything I'd hoped for and more, and I refuse to let Harlen ruin it for me.

The food is soon ready and the guests drift over. I grab some food, making room for the others, and go to stand near Alex. He's a keen young man and has great plans for the catering cabin. I'm happy to let him tell me about them, and his excitement is infectious.

At all times, I'm keenly aware of where Harlen is, too. I keep him in my peripheral vision and I can see that he's clocking me, too. We manage to stay about the same distance apart as the evening progresses, never getting any closer or further apart. But somehow, the effect is turning me on, this macabre dance we're doing.

CHAPTER 13

arlen

AFTER A WHILE I can't take it anymore. It feels like we're two large cats circling each other, trying to find a weakness, waiting for one to make the first move. The tension between us is pulsing with static electricity. As much as I hate it, my body has other ideas and just glancing his way, knowing he's looking at me, is enough to keep me in a semi-hard state.

Part of me wants to leave, but damned if I will. I missed the wedding reception because of him, so there's no way I'm bailing on this gathering, too. But I need a break. Mostly because I heard his laughter across the patio, and the sound of it made my jeans very uncomfortable. I turn away and head down a path, not with any direction in mind, just away, so no one can see me rearranging myself. I keep walking for a while, but when I get to the rose garden, I sink down onto a bench. I'll head back in a few minutes, but right now I just want to enjoy the peace and quiet.

My eyes drift over to the willow trees, and I contemplate whether to suggest that we need to start looking at some of them. Some willows, especially the crack willow, don't last all that long and are prone to breaking in high winds. I want to do a survey of them before winter so we can have a plan of what needs to be done. I'm so wrapped up in my thoughts, happy for my mind to be able to focus on something normal for once. Which is why I don't sense anyone approaching until they sit down next to me.

I immediately know who it is, and despite the thrill of having him this close, it really pisses me off. I'm trying to have a moment when he *isn't* in my thoughts. I'm finally succeeding, having a moment's respite from him, and here he comes, barging in when he isn't wanted.

Can the universe not just give me a break?

"Harlen?"

I ignore him and stare straight ahead, hoping that perhaps he'll go away. Then damn if he doesn't try again.

"Can we talk?"

Anger bubbles up, fairly irrational, but I'm done caring. I chance a glance at him. No Harlen, bad idea. Last time he was this close, I'd kissed him. I look away and say the first thing that comes into my head.

"Why don't you fuck off and go back to playing happy family. That's all you've ever wanted, isn't it? Or are you going to abandon them again this time, too?" I hear a sharp intake of breath, but don't wait for an answer. I don't want one. I jump up from the bench and stride in the opposite direction to the house. I don't feel like going back to join the party now. Fucking Duncan Blake ruining everything.

I start to head towards my car, but stop. I really don't want to go without saying goodbye to Jackson and Luca—again. So instead, I turn and head to the barbecue, hoping to make my exit brief. Keith catches me before I make it to where the rest of the guests are.

"Are you alright?" he asks, frowning at me. I guess I still look pissed off. I school my features into a more neutral state.

"I'm good, Keith. I just remembered I need to do something and was going to say bye to Luca and Jackson."

He looks like he's about to say something else, but then Duncan appears from the direction of the rose garden. I thought he would have made it back by now, but I guess not. He sees us and a look of pain flashes across his face. He spins round and heads off the other way. Keith looks between me and Duncan's retreating back. I force myself to keep my face neutral.

"I feel sorry for him," he says, watching Duncan's retreat.

"Sorry?" I try to keep the incredulity from my voice.

"To have been denied access to his children. It's nice he has this chance now."

"What?" I don't comprehend what Keith is trying to say.

"Jackson told me. That his mother had applied for a restraining order once she found out he was living with another man. He wasn't allowed to see or make contact with them at all."

"Huh?" It was the only word I could utter. If Keith noticed, he didn't acknowledge it as he continued.

"Poor guy. He loved those kids. He moved to the other side of the world to cope with it, as it broke him being so close but not being able to see them. That wife of his must have been a real piece of work."

I stop registering his words. Fuck. No wonder Duncan had looked so desolate at what I'd said. I'd struck a low blow. A *very* low blow. I'm still angry with him for what happened back then. But I thought he was a real shit, littering the world with broken hearts, then turning up like nothing had happened.

Maybe I was wrong. Maybe I was completely off the mark. I

feel shitty, and I certainly can't face him now, not after what I'd just said to him.

"Um, Keith?"

He turns to me.

"Can you send my apologies to Jackson and Luca and tell them I'll see them Thursday? There's something I need to do."

"Yeah, sure. You alright?"

"I'm fine, Keith. I'll see you soon," I reassure him. There's nothing I need to do, except be alone for a little while.

 uncan

I WATCH as Harlen pulls up next to my car. I'd got rid of the rental and purchased an SUV, much more suitable for the forest tracks to the site which I now own. The plans have been submitted, and it's just a matter of waiting, hopefully for approval. But there are some things I can do in the meantime, and one of those is to get a survey of the trees. Some will have to come down, but I'm hoping to minimise that. I also want an assessment for some of the others, regarding how to construct the house to keep from damaging their root system, and in turn, for them not to disrupt its foundations in the future.

I'm surprised that Harlen agreed to do this after the last time we'd seen one another. I had thought about using someone else for this, but Harlen is the best tree surgeon in the county. What would I say to Jackson or the rest of the community if I did that? I'm hurt by what he'd said—deeply hurt. As if I didn't have enough guilt about what had happened. It took a long time before I rejoined the other guests at the barbecue and I was glad that he'd gone. If I'm honest, if he'd still been there and had looked me in the eye as if nothing had happened, I definitely would have found someone else to advise me on this job.

As it is, I actually want him to explain himself, and hope I can explain my side, too. Is that his problem with me? He thought I was someone who would abandon his children? That's not the Harlen I knew, and I'd really like to know what's happened to him in the meantime. At least out here in the forest, there's no one else to interrupt us.

As he approaches, I decide to slip into professional mode. It might make it easier—especially for him not to stick the knife in again.

He looks wary though, uncertain. He's definitely not glowering at me, and I wonder if he's been told the truth. I've only spoken to Jackson, but I know that Luca also knows. It's Jackson's decision to tell anyone else he wants to know.

"Thank you for coming. Did you have a chance to look at the plans?"

"I did, and I must say this is going to be an impressive build." He looks away for a minute then takes a breath. "I'm sorry, Duncan."

Well, that's something. I mull it over for a few seconds. As he's brought it up, we might as well do this now.

"For what you said the other day, or for being a prick since I arrived?" I watch him wince. Good.

"For what I said. I was wrong, and it was out of order. I know the truth now, and I'm sorry."

So someone told him then, but what he'd said *really* hurt. He does genuinely seem sorry and I guess I have to move on from that—almost.

"Apology accepted." He looks relieved, but I'm not going to let him off that easily. "Why would you think I'd do that to my own children, abandon them like that?"

"I don't know. I wanted to think badly of you, I guess."

"Think badly of me. Why? What have I done?"

"Nothing," he says with a sigh. His shoulders sag and his face shuts down.

"Harlen, talk to me, please." The niggling feeling of something not being quite right is back.

"I thought you knew."

"Knew what?" I have no idea what the fuck he's on about. "You're going to have to spell it out for me."

"You must have known how I felt about you."

I think I might have opened my mouth like a fish. A wave of clarity washes over me and a thousand feelings crowd into my body. I exhale, trying to breathe round the huge knot that has lodged itself in my chest.

"Why didn't you say anything?"

He emits a sad sigh and looks away, staring out at the view as if he can't face me while he talks.

"Do you remember that night, just before our finals?"

"What, when you kissed me?" I pick that one, as it's been on my mind a lot. A tiny smile appears on his lips, but disappears again so quickly I wonder if I've imagined it.

"No. Well, yes. Please remember that night. But do you also remember the next night?"

I'm confused. It was so long ago that the timing from back then is just a blur, so I really don't know what he's talking about.

"Not specifically," I offer as an answer, and I see his face scrunch slightly as he swallows.

"The next night, you came round and told me Gloria was pregnant." He pauses. "You were so excited, but nervous too. I

61

remember you couldn't sit still, you didn't know what to do. You bounced around my flat like a ping-pong ball."

"Oh, was that the next day?" I remembered that occasion, but not when it was.

"Before you dropped your big news, I was going . . ." He stops and scrubs his hand down his face. Then he turns to look at me, his eyes glistening.

"I was going to tell my best friend that I was in love with him."

I watch him pause, needing to collect himself.

"I was going to tell him I'd been in love with him for a long time. I was excited when he told me he was bi and we kissed. Even though he said it was a mistake, I thought he may have said that because he believed I wanted to help him understand himself. But I held onto some hope that he might love me back. Because I felt something in that kiss, and was damn sure he felt it too."

"Why didn't you say anything?" My voice is barely a hoarse whisper.

"You'd just told me you were going to be a father. I knew how much you wanted that, and whatever I felt, I couldn't take that away from you."

"You could have said something." My mouth goes dry and I swallow to try to get some moisture back.

"How could I? I was so sure that you felt something for me, but when you came with your news, I felt so stupid for wanting you. Would it have changed anything?" His voice sounds pained, and he turns away from me.

"I don't know." I truly don't. I'm shocked at this revelation, and my thoughts are bouncing between back then and the last few weeks, trying to make sense of it.

"I'll tell you what would've happened." He raises his voice and starts pacing in front of me. "You'd have either gone anyway, and I'd have felt the rejection, or you could have missed out on being a father." He stops and faces me. His eyes are bleak, with decades of broken dreams and unspoken hurt. His voice cracks. "Duncan, I loved you too much to make you choose."

I feel stuck in time and space. I can't move. I can't form a single word right now. Not even a thought in my head.

He pushes past me and walks a little way away. Automatically, like a compass needle orienting on its true north, I slowly turn to watch him.

He rests a hand on a magnificent oak tree and looks up at it. When he speaks, his voice sounds almost normal, but I can hear the anguish in it.

"You know, I think we can keep this tree and work around it."

CHAPTER 15

*H*arlen

I HAVE to walk away so Duncan can't see the tears forming in my eyes. I bared it all to him. It should be a relief, but it isn't. The weight of it still hangs on my shoulders—except now he knows, and that somehow makes it worse. I feel hands on my shoulders, gently requesting that I turn round. I shrug them off and turn further away, clenching my fists.

I'm spun round, caught off guard by his roughness. Hands fist in my hair as he pulls me close so our foreheads touch, the tracks of his tears a mirror image of my own.

I try to break free, but he holds me fast, just staring at me. I don't touch him, and my only grip on reality right now is the pain from my nails digging into my palms. After a few long moments where he doesn't speak, he pulls me into a hug. His arms wrap round me, and he kisses into my hair whispering, "Harlen, Harlen, Harlen."

A sob escapes me, and I lean into him. I put my arms around him, tentatively at first, then stronger. But it's not enough. I need to be closer. I need him. I want to finally claim him as mine.

In that split second, when I draw back and meet his eyes, I see the same hunger reflecting back at me, oceans deep and eons old. Our lips crash together. It isn't soft and tender, but desperate and hungry. We gasp for air as teeth clash and tongues mesh, clinging to each other as if our lives depend on it, and it's still not enough. I kiss down his throat, messy and sloppy, but I don't care. I want to feel him. My hands try to work the buttons on his shirt but I fumble. The process is too slow and fiddly, so instead I lower my hands to his belt. That gives me little resistance, and as I undo the button and zipper on his jeans, I drop to my knees in front of him.

I pull them down roughly, along with his boxer briefs, freeing his cock, which juts out at me. It's long, not overly thick, but just perfect and rock hard. My own, that had been filling steadily, jerks at the sight of it, and I give it a few seconds of reverence that finally I'm going to taste him. I lap a bead of precum off the tip, savouring the salty taste before licking round his cockhead. Now I'm here, with what I've been waiting so long for in front of me, the desperation flows away and I want to take my time. I drag my tongue over his slit, hearing a sharp intake of breath which is replaced by a low moan as I suck him into me. I risk a glance and he's watching me, his lips slightly parted and his pupils wide within lustful irises. It's everything I've dreamed of and more, and now I want to devour every inch of him. I take more of him into my mouth, until my nose is buried into his thick, bushy hair. His scent fills my nostrils and it spurs me into action. I slurp and suck at him, sliding my tongue up the vein running along the underside of him.

Fingers tangle into my hair and he pulls my head back

slightly, stopping my motion and easing me halfway off him. I look up and see the question in his eyes.

God, yes. What he's asking sends a tingle down my spine, and my cock aches from being so hard.

I nod my assent, giving him permission to possess me, to wreck me. I feel him hit the back of my throat with every erratic thrust of his hips as I swallow my gag reflex. My drool mixed with precum dribbles down my chin, his balls slapping and spreading the wetness against me. I grab the back of his legs, mostly to keep myself upright from the punishing pace he's setting as he fucks my mouth, and I relish it. I can't get enough and want to be split in two by him.

I feel it, just as he's about to come, and don't let him draw back. I keep my lips locked round him as he spurts into my mouth and down my throat. I keep him there as he shudders to a stop and I take every drop before withdrawing, still licking my lips with the taste of him. I wipe my chin with my hand and rise to my feet. He's leaning against the tree, panting and looking so bloody gorgeous. I press a kiss to his glistening lips and turn away. I get a few steps before he calls out.

"Harlen?"

"I still hate you Duncan."

"I thought you said you loved me?"

"That too."

As I reach my Jeep, I turn back.

"Yes, you should definitely keep that tree."

His laughter still rings in my ears as I drive home.

uncan

DESPITE WHAT HARLEN SAID, and despite the best fucking blow job of my life, I knew deep down things weren't going to be that easy.

I'm not sure what I want, and I sure as hell don't know what Harlen wants; I don't think he even knows.

But at least now I understand. There's nothing I can do to change what happened. Would things have been different if he'd told me? Would we have explored things together or would I have still trodden the path I did? If I could time travel, would I go back and change it?

A random thought occurs, that if the past had been different then I might not have got to know Isabel and my grandchildren —even if I did wait a long time for that. Hell, Jackson might not even have been born, and the thought of that saddens me, leaving new grief lodging itself in my bones. No, I'm going to take the same approach as my wise-beyond-his-years son and say that everything has been for a reason. What the fuck the universe wants me to do now, though, I've no idea.

With a sigh, I turn away from the familiar cityscape in front of me and sit back down at my computer. Those thoughts are of no use to me right now. I'm no longer in Larchdown. Not long after I returned from the woods, Gavin called. It was very early in Australia, so it would have to be something serious for him to contact me. My heart dropped as I answered it, thinking something might have happened to Isabel or the kids. It wasn't that, and I had to take a minute to allow the hammering in my chest to stop, so it had taken a while for me to make sense of what he was saying. There had been an accident on a construction site. It was for a building that we'd designed the plans for. Whilst the fault lay in the safety procedures, or lack thereof, the construction contractors were deflecting bad press by trying to say the design required them to work in a certain way, and that had caused the accident.

It's all bullshit. But I didn't want Gavin to have to face it alone, so I flew back to Sydney on the next flight. Before I left, I called my lawyers to make sure they were briefed, and then had a more difficult conversation with the client. I'd advised them to use different contractors, but they hadn't heeded my warning, and I wanted to make sure that they knew where we stood.

Once I'd arrived in Sydney and had a shower, my next stop was to see the family of the poor guy who'd been in the accident. Some people might think that visiting them was some sort of admission of guilt, but I'm calling bullshit on that one, too. I knew the contractors would try to wheedle their way out of responsibility somehow, and while legal battles need to be fought, the family is the one who suffers the most. I gave them the contact for another lawyer I trusted, and told them to ask her to send the bills to me. It wasn't much, but it was a start.

. . .

AS THE SUN starts setting over the city and the lights start blinking into existence across the skyline, I decide to call it a day. Everything is as under control as it can be. I'm meeting with my lawyers in the morning and then holding a press conference in the afternoon. I sent Gavin home hours ago with a promise that I'd come see Isabel and the kids tomorrow. I know she's keen to hear about Jackson. I've been up for at least forty-eight hours straight. I huff a laugh, that what I'm doing now is a world away from when Harlen had left me in the woods with my jeans round my ankles and a sappy expression on my face. Was it only two days ago?

As I go to shut down my computer, an email pings into my inbox.

It's the report from Harlen on how to manage the trees at the site. I'll check the report later and add it to the documents on the planning portal. There's not much I can do until planning is approved, so it's just a waiting game for a month or so. I stare at the email before me. It doesn't say anything—nothing, not even my name or a greeting—just a standard business signature and the attachment. The absence of any communication speaks volumes. In the rush and the need to get things sorted quickly, I'd not told Harlen I was leaving, only managing a quick call to Jackson from the airport as my flight was being called. Not that I thought I needed to tell Harlen anything; it's not like we're together. I sigh at the screen, realising my mistake. The blank email is the biggest "fuck you" I could have received.

CHAPTER 17

*H*arlen

I THOUGHT I could get Duncan out of my system. That if I allowed myself a taste of him, it would alleviate the need. I was kind of hoping I'd discover I didn't need him anymore. It would certainly make my life a lot easier. But it doesn't, and the intensity of it doubles when I'm in his presence.

I had to walk away from him in the woods; I couldn't cope with the emotion. I didn't want him to see that I would have done anything to have him. Hell, I'd do anything just for him to glance at me. I hated that I was so desperate. I hated myself, and ultimately it made me hate him, even though I loved him at the same time.

But the spark of hope that I'd had, that little flame of a guiding light I'd been nurturing since Keith told me what Duncan had been through . . . A flicker I'd bravely allowed to flare when I bared my fucking soul to him.

He'd snuffed it out.

Within hours of me going on my knees to him, he's gone . . .

Again.

And he didn't even let me know . . .

PART II
SUMMER

CHAPTER 18

 uncan

"Do you love him?"

I shrug as I lift the bottle to my lips and take a swig.

"Dad, do you know that sometimes you can be the most infuriating person ever?" Isabel levels at me. She's probably not wrong.

Things have settled down with my client and the construction contractors. After a few weeks of them denying any liability, a visit from the workplace health and safety inspector had them caving. My company was in the clear, not that there had been any actual doubt, and the family is getting the support they're due. In a few days, I'm heading back to Larchdown.

Isabel is throwing a farewell barbecue for family, friends, and colleagues as I'm not planning on being back for a while this time.

After some deliberation, I'd decided to tell Isabel about Harlen. I could use some advice.

"So do you, or not?" Ah, she still wants an answer then.

"It's complicated."

"You asked for my help, but you're not giving me much to go on," she says with a sigh.

I give her the most honest answer I can.

"In truth, I don't know what it is. There are two sides to it. On one hand, it feels like a tectonic plate in my core has shifted, aligning something older and bigger than the both of us, but on the other hand, I feel like a tangled mess."

I don't know if the feelings I have are for the Harlen I remember, the open and adventurous Harlen of my youth, or for the prickly, sour, and haunted Harlen of today. Another pang of guilt shoots through me. I know I wasn't aware of what he was feeling at the time, though if I examine our time together back then, there were clues. Without realising or understanding it, I'd fallen for him. And, though it was his choice not to tell me about his feelings, the fact still remains that I'm the cause, albeit unknowingly, of how Harlen is now. That thought has given me some sleepless nights. Whilst I can't label what I feel right now, I have an overwhelming urge to try to reverse the damage and make him smile again.

I tell Isabel this and she regards me for a minute.

"Do you know what I think?" She doesn't wait for an answer. "I think you're scared."

"Scared?" I sound incredulous, but now she's voiced it, the reality of the word takes hold within my bones and I know that she's correct. I am afraid. Being scared means I'm invested in the outcome, and that nugget of knowledge seems to carry the weight of the world in it.

"If you truly want something, you need to reach out with both hands, hold it close, and never let go. No half-measures. No faltering. You have to believe in yourself because if you don't, no one else will."

I blink at her for a moment, and like I had with Jackson, I wonder how my children got to be so wise.

"Thanks love." I give her a hug and squeeze her tight as I'm going to miss her while I'm in the UK.

"If he's worth it, then go for it," she says as I eventually release her. Saying it and doing it are two different things, and at the moment I have no idea how I'm going to go about it. Especially as it's clear what he thinks of me right now.

~

"I'M SORRY, it's not much." I turn from the small, leaded window to glance at the handsome, blond-haired young man standing behind me in the doorway of the small room.

"It's fine, er, Charley, is it?"

"Yes." He looks relieved. The best I can call the cottage is quaint, possibly even charming, at a push. It's a world away from my apartment with its floor to ceiling windows looking out across the city. But it'll be enough, at least until my house is built. I've been back in Larchdown for a couple of days, and I want a better base and more space than the small room at the pub. So I've swapped that small room for, well, a collection of small rooms. Lilac Cottage is probably as old as the pub, also thatched. It consists of a kitchen, living room, and dining room on the ground floor. Then an ancient, narrow staircase to two bedrooms and a shower room on the first floor. At least it has modern facilities; I had visions of a brick outhouse in the yard outside.

"If you need it right away, I can get the last of my things out now," Charley explains, as we crowd into the slightly larger of the small bedrooms. Were people a lot smaller a few hundred years ago?

"Am I pushing you out? Pete said—"

"No, it's fine, I'm not staying here anymore." Charley's smile lights up the room with that statement. "I just haven't moved all my stuff out. I should have done it ages ago. This has done me a favour, really."

The cottage belongs to Pete, who owns the local garage and is, I understand, Charley's uncle.

"It'll be good for it to have someone in it again." Charley rests a hand against the old wooden door frame. "I don't think old buildings do well if they're empty."

I find myself agreeing with him as I follow him back downstairs. Old buildings which stand empty, even if they are maintained, don't seem to last as well as ones which have been almost constantly lived in. It's as if they breathe with the life of their inhabitants.

"Do you need a hand?" I ask, as Charley starts gathering a few things together.

"No, I'll be fine. Can you give me about an hour?"

"Sure. However long you need."

"Great. Come back then and I'll give you the keys."

I leave him to it. Instead of walking straight back to The Blacksmith's Arms, I wander along the riverbank for a little while. I'm in no rush and after the activity and stress of the last few weeks, it's a relief to slip into the slower pace of the village. I really missed it while I was in Australia. I smile at the thought of how much its influence has got under my skin in the short time I've spent here. Even though I'd only spent a few weeks here before going back to Australia for a while, coming back felt as comforting and familiar as settling into a favourite chair.

I admit some of my thoughts—okay a lot of my thoughts— in Australia had centred around Harlen. I haven't seen him or spoken to him since before I went away. I know what he thinks of me, but I'm hoping to change his mind.

CHAPTER 19

arlen

I HEAR the thunk of a drink being placed on the bar in front of me. I look up from where I've been staring into the bottom of an empty pint glass, deciding whether to have another one.

At first, I think it's Darla anticipating my thoughts and what my decision would be. But it's not a pint glass. It's a tall drink. It takes me a few seconds to recognise what it is. It's a Mexican Mule, and there's only one person who would know the signif-icance of that. I glance up at Darla, and she shifts her eyes and gives a barely perceptible tilt of her head towards the other end of the bar.

I stare at the drink again. Instantly I'm taken back to that summer, the last summer before everything went wrong. When I had a secret love for my best friend and we were young and free and just being in his company was enough. We laughed so much that summer, and I don't think I've laughed so freely and lightly since. I feel a smile force its way onto my face at the memory.

It was a picnic . . . I'm not sure whose idea it was to have a picnic, especially along the banks of the river. I mean, it was *the* place to go in the summer when the weather was good, so it was busy. But it didn't matter, as we just wanted to laze about and talk and occasionally read. Friends would wander by and we'd chat before they moved on again. We'd joked that picnics wouldn't be complete without *lashings* of ginger beer. He'd made sure I brought some, for the joke he'd said, but it was when he produced a bottle of tequila that it got interesting. So we sat on the riverbank, slowly getting drunk, and talking about everything and nothing. We'd shared our hopes and dreams . . . well, not all of them. I didn't confess to him then, and then by the time I wanted to, it was too late.

But I do remember the way he felt as we became drowsy from the sun and alcohol, and I dozed with an arm thrown over him, nestled into his side. He didn't complain, and it had felt so right. We fitted together so well. I release a sigh at the memory as it fades, and I'm faced with the reality that nothing turned out the way I'd planned. Yes, my work did, but in love? There are just the tattered remnants, and I'm angry that's all I have left.

I look over to where I know Duncan is sitting, watching my contemplation of the drink. It feels like a goad, like a taunt. I'm surprised by his expression, though. I expect to see his smug, cheerful countenance, but instead he looks anxious—nervous even. He wears it like ill-fitting shoes, but it means that Mr Oh-So Perfect is capable of something other than suave confidence. Good. Maybe he did get the message, but then maybe not, as he's here and not leaving me alone.

I stand from my stool at the bar and face him. I see a tiny spark of hope in his eyes. Too bad.

I'd sworn off spirits after the last time and I know I should leave it. Refusal of the drink would send him a clear signal. But I have absolutely no willpower when it comes to Duncan Blake, and I'm still angry at the memory of what I could've had being evoked. I'll show him what a little trip down memory lane means to me. I pick up the drink and down it in one go, fighting back a cough as the tequila burns my throat. With as much dignity as I can muster, I gently put the glass back on the counter, turn, and walk away.

"HARLEN?"

I'm halfway to my truck. The alcohol hits me when I get outside, and a part of me is registering that it wouldn't be a wise move to try to drive after that drink. I spin round.

"What do you want, Duncan?" I snarl.

"To start over."

It sounds so simple, those three little words, but it isn't.

"From where? The time you left to go make a family? The time you left the country to start over? Or the last month when you left without telling me?"

He winces at that, but he doesn't bite back and that angers me even more. I want to have an argument. I want to push him and see him snap. I want to see that calm, cool exterior crumble. I want to see if he's a mess inside like me.

"Can you drive?" He asks calmly.

"Probably not, but whose fault is that?" I retort loudly.

The smug bastard smiles slightly. I want to wipe that smile off his face; I just can't decide which I want to use more, my fist or my mouth.

"Look, I've rented a cottage across the green. I have coffee."

The rational part of my brain kicks in, that coffee actually wouldn't be a bad idea right now. I gesture for him to lead the way, and when he does, I amble along behind. One coffee and

I'll be okay to drive home. That's all I need, I reason with myself.

I've never been inside Pete's old cottage before. It's tiny, but solid and very charming. Duncan's six-foot-two frame takes up a lot of space in the small kitchen. I lean against one of the countertops and watch him make the coffee. To be honest, I'm getting an eyeful. In the pub—taking the drink and walking away—I wanted to give the same message as before. To stay away. It's the only way I can protect myself and my heart. But somewhere along the way that message got scrambled, and being this close to him is intoxicating. I know keeping my distance is the only way, but I screwed that up by following him into the kitchen. I could've accepted the offer of the drink and waited in the living room, but now I've got him in my sights, I don't want to let him out of them again.

We don't speak, and I don't move.

I just watch him work, appreciating how good his arse looks as he bends over to reach for something in a cupboard. I feel his breath on me as he reaches past to the fridge, and I catch the glance he gives me. I can't read his expression and I try to keep my face neutral. I'll have my coffee and leave, as that's the sensible thing to do. But then, I've never been one to heed reason.

When he stands in front of me holding out a coffee cup, I don't take it. I'm more interested in what else he has to offer. I lazily look down at the cup and back at him. I still make no move to take it. The seconds stretch. He raises an eyebrow. I'm still not going to give in. I slowly lick my lips and I see his eyes dart to them. I get a small thrill that he notices and my cock gives a twitch, but still I don't move.

His eyes darken, and something resembling a smile plays across his face before it flickers out. He puts the cup down on the countertop and steps closer to me. I stay still, but the act of him coming this close has me instantly sporting a semi.

He brackets his arms on either side of me and leans in, his lips close to my ear, and whispers gently.

"Are you going to have your coffee?"

His breath tickles the hairs on my neck and it tingles down my body, goosebumps rising on my skin. My semi has sprung to fully hard. My mouth feels too dry to speak, but I still want to push him. I give a little shake of my head.

"Hmmm." His mouth is still close to my ear. "What is it that you *do* want, then?" He shifts a leg, firmly pushing his thigh between mine. I have no defence against that and my breath hitches. I try—and fail—not to let out a small whine.

I feel his breath against my neck as he chuckles, fully aware of the effect he's having on me.

"No," is his simple response.

What? What does he mean?

He must have felt me tense as he continues.

"Oh, I want you Harlen." These are much better words. His mouth is against my throat—not kissing, just whispering—and it's sending me into a frenzy, my cock pushing against my zipper.

"I want you laid out on my bed. I want to see you ready for me to fuck you into next week."

Finally, we're in agreement about something.

"Please," I utter. My neediness is embarrassing, but I'm past caring. Now I've got this far, I want it all.

I move myself against him to try to get some friction, to relieve some of the aching in my cock.

"But not like this," he growls against my neck.

I wish I knew what he meant. His words are negative, but the feeling of him being pressed up against me and his hot breath are making me dizzy with lust. I'd do anything for him right now. His breathing is ragged; surely he's feeling this, too. All it would take is for me to make one move, and yet I don't. He rests his forehead on my shoulder for a second. Then, with another "no," that sounds almost like he's saying it to himself rather than me, he pulls back and breaks contact. My body is bereft and I don't like it at all. His face is blank as he retreats to the other side of the kitchen.

"Duncan, what the fuck?" I demand.

"Drink your coffee," he commands. And after a scowl at him I obey, but only because I think he might tell me what just happened.

The coffee is half-cold, but that means I can gulp it down in one go. I put down the cup and wipe my mouth with the back of my hand.

"What the fuck just happened?"

He picks up his own cup and takes a swig. Then he holds it in front of him, cradling it in both hands like it's some sort of shield.

He takes a breath.

"I think we should get to know each other first."

"We *do* know each other. You're my oldest friend," I protest plaintively, still miffed that he's just refused me. I adjust myself, as my dick is uncomfortable without a strong thigh to rub against.

"Harlen, I'm planning to live here, make this my home. Christ, I'm building a house here. I would really like you to be a part of that new life. A big part. But I feel like I don't know you, not this you. We can't expect to pick something up after thirty years. I want to do this properly. I don't want to mess this up for a quick fuck."

"A quick fuck?" In my anger, this is the only thing I can focus on, and I don't process the rest of it. "Is that all you think I am?"

"Harlen, that's exactly what I'm not saying." His jaw tenses like he's going to snap, but is holding it together. For some reason—maybe due to the unreleased sexual tension, or maybe just because I'm fucked up and he's being all calm and mature

—his words start to sink in. I step up to him, this time crowding into his space.

"Maybe a quick fuck is all I want from you."

It's a complete lie, of course, but I don't really know if I can offer him any more than that. To give him what he wants scares the hell out of me.

His shoulders sag a little and the light dims in his eyes. I've crossed a fucking line. I can't just stop, can I? He doesn't say anything more, he just looks a little sad. Way to go, Harlen, you big, fucked up mess. But I'm not sure if I can do what he's asking. Why would he even want me, anyway? I'm pretty sure he won't want the real me once he knows it all. And to make sure, I give him my parting shot.

"I never figured you would be a prick tease," I snarl, and turn around. Walking away seems the only thing to do. To put distance between us. As every time we get close to each other, it gets messy.

CHAPTER 20

 uncan

SLEEP DOESN'T COME easy once Harlen leaves. It could have gone better, a lot better. The drink was supposed to be a peace offering, a reminder of better times. I hadn't wanted to start anything with him tonight. It was just supposed to be a simple coffee for me to say I'm sorry. But when he stood there challenging me, daring me, I desired him badly. And, while perhaps I should have taken what he offered, it took all my powers of restraint not to. I'd meant what I'd said about wanting to get to know him first, but I don't know if he really believed that or wants that himself. All I'm left with is an aching boner and the feeling that I've made things worse.

I try to recall Isabel's words, but they don't help much except to galvanise me into giving it another try. Hoping that somehow I can reach the real Harlen, who I know is still inside. I want to get past the snarly exterior that snaps like a cornered animal. I want him to remember who he is, too. But until then, I'll be whatever I need to be for him.

By MORNING, I'm tired and cranky. I don't think I managed more than a couple of hours of sleep. The heaviness that I felt last night after Harlen left still sits queasily in the bottom of my stomach.

I make sure I have a dose of strong coffee before I tackle my emails. I have a few from Gavin; everything is going fine in Australia, and I schedule a call with him for later in the week for a catch up.

I'm returning to my makeshift desk in the dining room with my second coffee when I hear an email notification ping. A glance tells me it's from the planning office. I'd amended some of the plans, so I'm surprised they've reached a decision so quickly.

I hesitate before opening it, my hand hovering over the mouse. I recognise it as nerves. Why do I feel nervous? I hadn't realised that this meant so much to me. Having a base in the UK, being near Jackson, this amazing community which makes me feel like I've lived here forever. I don't dare let my thoughts turn to any more than that; surely that's enough for one person to need, and it should be, but I know I want more.

I take a deep breath and click the email, releasing it in a whoosh as I read the words, "planning approved."

I feel so relieved I almost start shaking, and I feel the need to tell someone. I instinctively pick up the phone and call Jackson. He sounds as excited as I am and he invites me up to the house later for dinner to celebrate. My next job is to contact the building contractors to finalise the plans and see when they're available. I know that good companies are in great demand, and these are the best in the area, so I hope they can start soon. I make arrangements to meet with the CEO at the site in a couple of days.

I work steadily, until my stomach growls and I realise that lunchtime passed hours ago. I get up and stretch out my limbs. The dining room chairs in the cottage aren't ideal for sitting on for hours, but if I had the usual office chair I use, it would take up so much space I'd barely get in and out of the room. I had thought about renting an office space, especially for running the UK office, but as I've designed one into the new house, it seems pointless. I can put up with the cramped conditions for a while longer.

I make some toast to stop the hungry noises, and head into the living room to do some proper stretches and yoga. I've been neglecting it a little lately and I know that at my age you need to work harder just to stay still. I squeeze in another hour's work before shutting off my computer and heading up to see Jackson.

It's a beautiful summer's day and the late afternoon sun is still high in the sky; it'll be a few hours before the sun sets. Jackson greets me with a big hug.

"That's great news, Dad! I'm happy you want to stay here."

I revel in his hug a little, the simple human contact comforting me as I understand how on edge I've been for the last few weeks. With setting up a presence in the UK, the Australian incident, waiting for news on the planning, and . . . No, I'm not going to think about him right now. Everything else is going so well. I don't want anything to detract from that.

"I've just got a few things to finish up out here, but you can head into the house if you want. Luca's cooking tonight. He's been desperate to try out a new recipe, and when I said I'd invited you, he jumped at the chance."

"Sounds good." From what I'd heard from Jackson, Luca had hardly cooked before they met, but had got more adventurous and found a love of cooking. "But I can help you out if you want."

"Thanks, I just need to move a few of these pots to the greenhouse. But there's some wood to be moved from the avenue, and a couple of pieces still to chop if you're ok doing that."

It's a good job that I haven't dressed especially for dinner; I know better than that by now, though I'm not dressed for garden work either. I load a few of the logs into the waiting wheelbarrow and pick up the axe.

"You're doing that all wrong."

I spin round at the voice, the axe still in my hand. Harlen grabs the axe just before it connects with his head.

"See. Doing it wrong." He smirks.

"Shit, Harlen! You shouldn't sneak up on a guy like that."

He wrenches the axe off me.

"Let me show you how it's done." I gesture with my hands for him to go ahead. "I mean, you're hardly dressed for it." His tone is mocking. When I look at him, he grins at me and it's feral. I guess he's still mad at me.

He makes quick work of the few logs that are left. I enjoy watching his muscles ripple and flex, though he attacks the wood as if it bears him a grudge. I have to admit, I'm kind of sad when he's finished. He straightens up and the smile he shoots me this time looks genuine. I finish putting the last of the logs with the rest and face him. My eyes flick to his throat as he swallows, and I know I should say something, but I'm not sure what. He looks like he might be wrestling with the same thoughts. The air fizzles between us and I ought to break it somehow. Instead, I take a step towards him and I see a look of knowing amusement cross his face.

I take another step.

"Thanks, Dad. Oh, hi Harlen. I didn't realise you were still here."

Harlen turns to Jackson, who is walking towards us. I rapidly take a few steps back, wondering how much Jackson saw. If he had seen anything, he doesn't mention it or look at us as if anything is out of the ordinary.

"I was just finishing up and thought I'd lend a hand." He gestures with the axe he's still holding.

Jackson looks over, and I shrug.

"He didn't give me much of a choice."

As Jackson turns back to Harlen to thank him, I head towards the wheelbarrow to start moving the logs.

"Well, thanks Harlen. Do you want to stay for dinner?"

Harlen looks over at me. His face closes down, and his tone is cold. "Maybe another day. I wouldn't want to intrude on some family time."

I grasp the wheelbarrow handles and head off towards the log pile. As I get further away, I hear Jackson trying to change Harlen's mind. I guess he hasn't managed to, as when I return and head to the house, there's no sign of him.

"Hi . . . Dad." Luca's slight hesitation over calling me that, as if the word is somehow foreign to him, is so sweet and endearing. I smile at him. I don't know how anyone could have treated him so badly.

"Hi Luca. Something smells delicious."

He beams back at me and tells me about the pasta dish he's created.

"Wait, you made the pasta as well?" I'm impressed.

He gives a self-effacing shrug. "It's not that hard."

Right then Jackson appears, looking like he's just showered. He walks up to Luca and wraps his arms around him while he's standing at the stove, dropping a kiss on his head. I love the easy way they have with each other. Jackson catches me watching them as he turns round, and with a wink at me, he reaches past Luca to snag something out of the pan before dropping it into his mouth.

"Hey, no stealing," Luca admonishes with a laugh.

"I need to know if it's edible. We have a guest." That earns him a glare and a dismissal to go be useful by setting the table.

Jackson drags me off to the dining room, and I'm pressed into laying out the place settings while he fetches some wine.

The conversation over dinner—which is delicious—is easy. Luca is a man of many talents. They're both so pleased to hear that the planning application has come through, and demand to be taken up to the site as soon as possible. I'm pleased with their enthusiasm and can't wait to show them the house plans as well. After dessert and coffee, I'm feeling tired and decide to head back to the cottage. A couple of months ago, I would never have dreamed I'd be having a fabulous dinner with my son and making plans like this. It fills me with a sense of pride and contentment.

CHAPTER 21

*H*arlen

"WILL you be at The Arms later?" Keith asks, as I pop into the bakery on Friday morning.

"I might be," I give as my non-committal answer, to which Keith just grunts. I know what he thinks of me, spending my time like some hermit in my cabin in the woods. But that's how I like it. That's why I live out there. I like the peace and quiet and the freedom to please myself. I know Keith is gregarious and loves to be surrounded by people, to be in the heart of everything, and usually organising it. But that's not me.

"We miss seeing you." He tries again as he hands me the flapjack I'd ordered. In truth, I haven't joined them for several weeks and I think it wouldn't hurt to show my face occasionally, even if it is just to keep them off my back.

"You win. I'll see you all later," I call as I leave, and I hear Keith give a delighted guffaw behind me.

· · ·

MOST OF THE usual Friday night crew have arrived by the time I get there. I almost didn't bother. I'd been in the workshop and had forgotten the time. It's late by the time I finish up and I debate whether to bother, but knowing Keith, I'll never hear the end of it. So after a quick shower, I drive down to the village. I head to the bar first and get a drink before anyone can order for me. I know my choice will probably invite comment but I hope not too much. I grab my bottle of zero alcohol beer and head to the table. I'm trying to stay dry for a while. Some of my poor decisions lately have been fuelled by alcohol, and I want to try to do better. If I can, then maybe, just maybe, there might be some hope for me.

Everyone is sitting arranged in a rough circle, so I pull up a chair and join them. I look up and realise that I'm sitting opposite Duncan. He gives me a faint smile, but doesn't say anything. Keith looks at my drink, knowing I usually have a pint, but when I meet his eyes he just gives me a nod. When he gets up a few minutes later, he gives my shoulder a squeeze as he passes. Somehow that feels worse. Am I so fucked up that he notices the attempt to clean up or is he just being his usual, supportive self? Who knows with Keith? Sometimes I swear that guy has a sixth sense.

I join in the conversation, and it feels okay to be in this close group of friends. They're able to rib and joke as much as anyone, but they're never unkind or cruel. I guess most of them have gone through their own hardships, and they know not to push someone else.

Talk turns to Duncan's new house and that he'd received planning permission. I didn't know that, and a part of me is annoyed that I wasn't told. I know I'm being peevish and I haven't been approachable—quite the opposite, in fact. I have no claim on Duncan, and I've made that pretty clear. Still, I find myself glancing at him often, but I don't want him to notice, so I try to relax and engage in the discussion. When talk turns to other subjects, Duncan gets up and heads to the bathroom. I go to the bar to get another round. When he returns, I feel him settle on the stool and rest his forearms on the bar next to me.

"What will you have?" I ask.

"The same as you," he drops casually.

I feel my face settle into a frown as I stare at him.

"You know what I'm drinking?"

"I do."

"Oh." It throws me a little, but I order him the same just to see if he's serious. When Darla puts it on the bar, he takes a swig from the bottle.

"Why?" I ask as he places it back down. He looks at me, and instead of the usual sunny countenance, I see an expression a thousand fathoms deep. He turns away and fiddles with the label on the bottle.

"Solidarity," he states plainly. "Someone did it for me once, and it helped, knowing I wasn't alone."

This is the first time Duncan has shown me anything darker than his super-calm, upbeat character. The first time he's hinted that he too might have ridden the inner demons. I think back to what Keith told me, about what had happened with Duncan's marriage and his children. How I'd always thought he just moved on when things got too hard. I realise that is exactly what I've been waiting for him to do—to move on, to find me too difficult—and I've continually pushed him away to make it easier for him and for me. I should say thank you. I should be pleased that he's recognised me and is reaching out. Instead, I do what I always do when I can't cope with what I'm feeling at the moment. When it feels like way too much.

"Thanks, but I think I'm big enough to take care of myself." I stride back to the group to deliver their drinks.

Duncan doesn't join us; he stays sitting at the bar, drinking his drink. I'm hyperaware of him behind me, just sitting there. After a few minutes, Keith goes to talk to him. I can hear a murmur of their conversation and a low laugh, but Keith returns without him and he doesn't look at me, so I can only hope Duncan wasn't saying anything about me to Keith.

Darla calls last orders and we finish up our drinks. As I stand to leave, I see Duncan hasn't moved from his place at the bar, though he has been chatting with Darla. I feel a little guilty about what I'd said to him, but also pleased he wasn't sitting alone the whole time.

I head out the door to my truck, for once completely sober. Not that being sober has made me less of an arsehole, obviously.

"Harlen."

I stop at the sound of my name and slowly turn to see Duncan a few yards away.

"Do you want to come over to mine? For coffee?"

He offers it so genuinely, so sincerely, as if a short time ago I hadn't snubbed him and his kindness. I really can't fathom why he keeps doing this, why he keeps offering me another chance. He's standing under a streetlamp. The diffused glow settles around him like he's the only thing to be seen. A beacon in the darkness, something to focus on when everything is black. Maybe he could be my guiding light; my way back home.

I swallow, and decide to be the most honest I've been with myself since he reappeared in my life.

"Not yet."

CHAPTER 22

uncan

"AND YOU CAN START in two weeks?" I ask the woman in front of me, Kayla. She heads up the construction company I've chosen to build the valley house. I'm surprised they could fit in such a large build so quickly.

Kayla Brown, CEO of Brown Associates (Construction) is a good-looking woman in her forties. She's on the tall side of average with glossy auburn hair that lands on the shoulders of her immaculately tailored grey suit.

"The way I see it, Mr Blake, this build is interesting and could be very good for our portfolio. Likewise, having yourself as a client could be useful. We would hope that if we can build a house that you would live in, you might be more inclined to recommend us to your clients." She smiles reassuringly, and I like her business style. I have to admit, I like the preferential treatment as well, but I have to ask another question.

"You aren't putting another project back because of mine?"

If a company is willing to shift things around to accommodate clients at the expense of other jobs, I know that one day that could be me. I'd prefer to have a delay and know the company is trustworthy.

"There's been an unexpected hold on one of our projects; some Roman remains were found and until the archeologists have surveyed the area, we cannot continue. From previous experience, we know this can take several months, so we're able to fit your project in. We'll need two weeks to finalise the project plan, order the equipment, and commission the materials."

"Thank you, I appreciate it." I've dealt with several construction companies in the past, and the professionalism of Brown Associates impresses me. Kayla stands and as I make to stand as well, she gives me an amused smile.

"No need to get up, Mr Blake. If you could wait here for a moment, I want to introduce you to your project manager."

I settle back down and watch as she heads out of the office. The wall and door are all glass, so I can see her walk across the open-plan space to stop at a desk. She says a few words to the woman sitting there. She glances over at me, excitement etched on her face. She jumps up, grabbing a large folder before following Kayla back to the office. She's a couple inches shorter than Kayla and looks to be in her late twenties. Her black hair is pulled up into a bun, and large glasses frame her green eyes.

"Mr Blake, I'd like you to meet Holly Vance. She'll be the project manager for your build."

"Pleased to meet you, er, Miss, Ms . . ."

"Holly is fine." She thrusts out her hand for a shake. I take it and she grips mine before quickly releasing it, as if that was the minimum time required for social niceties. "As soon as I saw the plans for your house, I knew I wanted to be a part of it. It's just so interesting and innovative. The way it appears to grow out of the side of the valley, and the middle section that looks like the rest is floating. It's inspiring." She speaks quickly and I have to listen carefully to keep up. She pauses to draw breath and before she speaks again, Kayla interjects.

"Holly has a few questions, Mr Blake. Could I get you a drink? Tea? Coffee?"

I accept a coffee and then Holly spreads out the plans and work she's done so far, and rapidly fires off questions at me.

She's asking all the right questions, and even a few that make me think a little. She has made a very detailed project plan, and I'm pleased with how thorough she is.

I have a couple of questions for her as well, which she answers to my satisfaction.

"So," says Kayla, who's been sitting in on the meeting, listening to everything. "If you're fully happy for us to proceed, Mr Blake, then there are just a couple of documents to sign and we can get things in motion to break ground in two weeks."

It's all done very smoothly and as I sign my name, I feel excitement at seeing this project come to life. More so than all of my previous ones, because this build means so much to me. This one will be *my* home.

The good mood stays with me as I exit the office onto the busy Oxford city street. I stand looking round, deciding where to go next, when I spy a familiar face across the street. I jog across the road.

"Harlen?"

He turns at the sound of my voice. Do I see a little spark of something in his eyes? If I do, it's gone quickly.

"Duncan."

Now he's in front of me, I don't know what to say.

"Do you . . . Erm, I'm going to grab some lunch. Will you join me?"

"Yeah, okay." He gives a little shrug, like it's no big deal. I blink at him a couple of times. Honestly, I'm surprised by my asking and even more astonished that he agreed.

"Great." I look around wildly. I barely know Oxford and certainly have no idea where to go. "Could you recommend somewhere?"

That earns me an amused look and I like it. What I would give to see him laugh again.

"Come on, I know a place." He heads off along the street, and I have to walk quickly to catch up. It isn't far and before long, he heads towards a small building standing next to a large church. We enter the open door to a bustling little café, but my eyes are drawn upwards to an amazing vaulted ceiling. I'm not allowed to gawk for long as more people want to enter, so Harlen pulls me along to the counter. I'm still wide-eyed when he nudges me to get my attention, and I realise that I was asked a question.

"Er, sorry, could you repeat that?"

The server looks a bit frazzled as she asks again what I'd like. I make my selection from the board behind her, and we shuffle along to the next station to get our drinks and pay.

"Hi Marcy." Harlen greets the woman behind the till and she smiles widely.

"Hey Harlen, good to see you. It's been a while. I'll tell Will you dropped by."

"Thanks. Tell him I'll come round next week and sort those conifers. I know I promised to do it a while back."

"He'll be pleased." She smiles again, and I watch the exchange with surprise. Though why I should, I don't know. Maybe the fact is that Harlen smiles and seems at ease with her in a way I haven't seen before. He's certainly never seemed so relaxed when I've been around.

I ask for sparkling water and pay for us both, being treated to the same wide smile.

"Friend?" I ask, as Harlen leads us to an empty table and we sit down. His easy manner has receded slightly and his expression is guarded.

"I've known them for a good few years. Will and Marcy started this place, and I did some work for them on some trees out in the garden area. But I also take care of some at their home, too."

"So, do you come here often?" As soon as it's out, I realise it sounds like an extremely corny pick-up line for which I receive a slight quirk of the mouth—well more of a wince if I'm honest —and then a deadpan.

"Often enough." Now that I don't have people jostling me, I can take my time to stare again at the building.

"It's fourteenth century," Harlen explains. "It was a congregation house. The café has been here for about twenty years and is known for its sustainability. It sources a lot of local produce, much of it organic. They get some vegetables from Tom Walker's farm."

Just then, our food arrives, and it looks delicious. We tuck in, and after a few mouthfuls Harlen stops for a drink.

"Have you been to Oxford much?" he asks.

"Actually, no. This is my first time, but I'd like to see more of it." It's the truth, as what I have seen has piqued my curiosity for the ancient city. "I was finalising the construction plans for the house."

He hesitates only slightly before asking.

"They can start soon, then?"

I tell him of my meeting and how soon the build will start. He asks a couple of questions and I'm pleased that he sounds interested. The meal is over all too soon, and I feel we should leave, as there are people waiting for tables. With the food as good as it is, it's no wonder the café is so popular. We stand and Harlen heads back over to the till while I hover nearby. He says a few words to Marcy, then leans down and kisses her cheek.

She flicks a glance at me before saying something to him, to which he chuckles and shakes his head.

I sigh, knowing it'll be a long while before he's that relaxed around me. But I have seen glimpses of the old Harlen, and this is probably the longest time we've spent together without it ending snarly and bitter. It's certainly the longest conversation we've had since I've been back.

I've enjoyed spending some time with him and I don't want it to end just yet, but I have no reason I can think of to detain Harlen any longer. And to be fair to him, he did change his plans to come and have lunch. But we don't part, and end up walking down a street, almost aimlessly, though we aren't talking. I wonder if he's feeling the same as I am. We come to an impressive tower, and I look up at it. A sudden flash of memory presents itself to me.

"Do you remember the tower in the town square?" I ask. Where we went to university, the town square had a clock tower. Not as large as the one in front of us, but still impressive.

"I remember you daring me to climb it." I *had* done that. He'd been boasting of how they'd learnt to climb trees safely as part of his course, and one drunken Friday night I'd dared him to climb the clock tower. It was idiotic and dangerous, but we were young and stupid.

"I remember you managed it." He had, but how he didn't end up injured or worse, I'll never know.

"Do you recall, I challenged you to try it?" His voice sounds softer somehow, as if the memory is mellowing him slightly.

"Yes, and I tried, but I didn't get far." As I recall, I'd got stuck.

"But you tried."

I stare up at the tower in front of me. "I was petrified," I own up. I don't mind heights, as in tall tower blocks, but being exposed to the possibility of one's own demise is a different thing altogether.

"I think that was the first time I realised I was in love with you." It's a murmur and I hardly hear him. When I look at him, he's staring straight at me, his expression soft. Then he looks away for a few seconds, and when he turns back, his face looks like that was painful for him to say.

"I should go. I have a few things I need to do."

My chest feels empty, like I have no breath and I can't speak, so I just nod. As I watch him walk away, I'm wondering if we're better or worse off than we were before.

CHAPTER 23

arlen

So, I am able to spend some time in the company of Duncan without making a fool of myself. I can meet with him and not throw myself at him or say something that pushes him further away. Now that I'm over the first hurdle, I can see him with a sense of equilibrium.

That's bullshit.

If I believe that, then why am I standing outside Duncan's cottage one evening, just staring at the door?

I don't know what I want from him, I just know that I can't stay away. I thought that by agreeing to have lunch with him, doing something normal and on neutral territory, I could quench the yearning inside of me. But if anything, it's made it worse. I knock on the solid wooden door.

He opens it looking like an absolute vision, dressed in a t-shirt and sweatpants. Fucking sweatpants. I don't think I have any defences against that sight.

"Harlen, is everything alright?" He frowns and looks past me as if he might see the answers there, or if maybe I'm not alone.

"Is that coffee still on offer?" I manage. Duncan regards me for a brief second.

"Sure." He stands back to let me pass him in the narrow hallway. He smells citrusy and clean, with a hint of something richer underneath, sandalwood maybe. My senses are reeling slightly, and I use them as my excuse for blurting out.

"I haven't been drinking, if that's what you think."

He shuts the door and holds up his hands.

"I didn't say anything."

I realise that I've gone on the attack already. I take a deep breath to calm myself. Maybe this wasn't such a good idea after all. I'm not ready for this, for being this close to him, alone, especially in goddamn sweatpants. Maybe only public meetings —in the daytime—for a few months first, and I won't lose it the moment he stands so close to me. Now I'm here, though, I can at least try to have a coffee, instead of running away.

"I'm sorry," I mumble.

Duncan nods an acknowledgement and heads towards the kitchen. He fills the kettle and turns round, leaning back against the counter and crossing his arms.

"I *am* curious as to why you're here, though. Not that I'm not pleased to see you. I am—very pleased. But what is it you want, Harlen?"

I resist the urge to take the two steps I would need to close the gap between us. To press myself against him, push him back against the units, and suck bruises onto his skin. I fist my hands to keep them by my side and will myself to stay still.

"Coffee." What on earth did I say that for?

He smirks slightly. So he's not going to make this easy for me then. I can't blame him.

"You don't have coffee at home?"

"No, and the shop's shut," is my smart-arse answer.

I can see the light dancing in his eyes, and he smiles as he finishes making the coffee.

This time, instead of trying to hand me the mug, he sets it down on the counter next to me and leans in a little before saying, "Here's your coffee. I can give you some to take away if you've run out. If you need anything else, you're going to have to ask for it."

Then he walks past me and into the living room.

He's sitting in a large comfortable armchair, a standard lamp shining light over him. I notice a book on the side table next to him. He was probably reading before I came and disturbed him with my lame excuses. He waves a hand towards the couch to invite me to sit down. I do, but I perch on the edge. He takes a sip of his coffee and watches me. He looks calm, but I can see how set his jaw is. I guess I hadn't thought past this point. I didn't have a plan, just that I needed to see him, and now that I'm here I don't know what to do. I sure as hell can't do small talk.

The seconds stretch, and I hate this feeling. We never had this problem when we were friends at uni. Maybe this was a mistake. I remember we used to have silences, times when we wouldn't talk, yes. We didn't need to back then, we just enjoyed each other's company. Usually, we'd sit sprawled across each other, or at least close by. But of course, that was when he didn't know how I felt about him. The memory evokes a good feeling in me and I want to try to see if we can do that again. No, I want a whole lot more; I want Duncan in my bed. I want a relationship. I also know that he's offered the chance for it, I just need to reach out and grasp it.

He's still watching me, and I feel like when I finish my coffee, he might just ask me to leave. I take a gulp of my drink to try to calm my mind. I place the mug down on a side table.

I try to form the words. My palms suddenly feel sweaty and I rub my hands down my thighs.

"I want . . ." The words stick. I know this is what I want, but I just can't seem to let go of my safety net of protecting myself —protecting my heart—like I have for thirty years. I glance at him, but he hasn't moved. If anything, his eyes have got darker, and it's oh-so sexy. If I want to see those eyes forever, I need to say the next bit. I try again.

"I want to start over, too."

He doesn't say anything for a minute. At least he doesn't throw it back at me like I did to him. I twist my hands nervously, unable to look at him.

He rises from the chair and stands in front of me. I look up then, and he holds out a hand to me. I'm confused but I take it, and he hauls me to my feet. We stand toe to toe and, as usual with being this close, I can't control the effect he has on me. All the blood rushes to my cock, which leaves me feeling light-headed. My stomach churns and I open my mouth to say something, but for the life of me, I don't know what. I can't even remember my own name right now.

He places a finger on my lips, and with a little shake of his head whispers, "Shhh."

Then he pulls me out of the room with him and up the narrow stairs to his bedroom.

He starts unbuttoning my shirt. Is this really going to happen? Something that I've waited so long for? I've thought about this in my dreams—many times and in *many* different ways. Not quite like this, though.

"Du—"

He covers my mouth with his in a searing kiss that steals my breath away. He pulls back slightly.

"No talking," he commands, and looks at me. I nod my assent. He smiles and pulls my shirt off. He runs a hand over my chest, trailing a finger down my abdomen.

"Take these off." He gestures to my jeans and heads over to the dresser by the bed. He takes out a bottle of lube and a condom.

"I'm clean," I say. "I get tested regularly." I do, but also omit the fact that I haven't had sex in, well, a long time.

He doesn't turn around. "I said no talking." He sounds gruff, then continues in a softer voice. "But thank you for letting me know. I got tested recently, and I take it that as you mentioned it, you're ok with that?"

He looks at me over his shoulder, and I nod. I'm fully naked, as he asked. His eyes travel down my body and alight on my erection. His eyes widen and he looks at it hungrily. Stalking his way back over to me, he licks his thumb and rubs it over the end, smearing precum with it. A moan escapes and he chuckles. He takes hold of my hand again and gently leads me over to the bed.

"Lie down on your back." I do as he says and watch as he pulls his t-shirt over his head. I'm treated to a view of his chest that has a smattering of hair, but not much. It does, however, trail down to disappear beneath the waistband of his sweatpants, which are now tented with his own arousal. He pulls them down and his cock bounces as it's released. He takes them off and kneels on the bed, reaching for the lube.

And it's at that point my brain decides to intervene.

A swarm of thoughts buzz round my head . . .

Why is he doing this? What does he see in you? You're a fucked up mess, Harlen. He's just humouring you because you practically begged him the other day. And here you are, showing up and begging him again. What else were you doing on his doorstep? You said you want to start over and to try to do this, but he saw straight through you. He saw you haven't got what it takes to commit to anything. He saw that you just wanted to get fucked. He saw how needy you were. He feels sorry for you.

"I don't want your pity fucks," I spit out, jumping up and heading towards the door.

Before I can take a breath, I'm thrown face down on the bed, a knee digging into my back and an arm across my shoulders, holding me down. I struggle to get free, but he pushes harder. Who knew he was so strong?

He grabs a handful of my hair and pulls my head back, growling into my ear.

"Who said I was pity-fucking you?"

His voice is sending shivers down my spine and the vice-like grip he has me in is making my body feel . . . alive.

My brain is spiralling but my body is responding to his roughness, and I want it. *This* is what my body craves.

"That's all I am to you," I goad, and he drags my head back further, exposing my neck. My cock is rock hard and I wriggle, trying to get some friction under him. He digs his knee in a little harder.

"Oh, no you don't. You'll do what I say and you'll come only when I tell you to."

I whimper, and he releases his grip slightly, but that's not what I want. I want him to do more, hurt me more, make me feel . . . *more*.

"Like to see you try," I taunt.

He growls, and the noise blankets me in a heat that engulfs my senses.

He clamps his teeth down on my shoulder, marking me. He's already marked my soul. I want him to mark my body, too.

"Nnnggghhh," I moan. Fuck, I nearly come from that despite him saying I can't.

"I'm fed up with your self-pity. I'm sad that you've had it bad. I'm sorry that I was the cause of that, but you didn't tell me, and that's on *you*."

He licks the spot he had his teeth in a minute ago, and my body jerks as every nerve ending tingles. It feels so good.

"Now then." His breath sends warm tendrils winding round my neck. "Are you going to take your head out of your arse long enough for me to fuck it?"

CHAPTER 24

 uncan

HARLEN NODS and I release my grip on him. He could easily break free from my grasp; he hefts large pieces of wood all day long and I've seen him wielding an axe.

I knew what he wanted when I saw him standing on my doorstep, even if he didn't know it himself. I'd given him space to come to me. To take that first step.

The next step is mine, and it's what we both need to move forward.

The mark on his shoulder is blooming, and I have an intense feeling of satisfaction about that. I want to do it more. I shift my weight and remove my knee from the small of his back. I rub the spot gently as the blood flows back before raking my nails down his spine. He shudders and a breathy whimper escapes his mouth. The sound does things to me I haven't felt in a long time and makes me want to elicit a thousand moans from him.

I get my first reward as I dig my fingers into his arse cheeks, pulling them apart. He groans and bucks his hips. I want to spend hours getting to know every inch of his body, but right now I want to bury myself so deep in him, he sees stars for days.

"Can't fuck it just by looking at it."

Instinctively, I smack a red mark across his backside and when I hear a low chuckle I know that, whilst he might be at my mercy, he's got me right where he wants me, too. I grab his hips and haul him to his knees. I can't resist sucking a bruise onto one cheek while running a finger firmly down his crack. He hisses a "yes" at me. I reach for the lube and coat my fingers. He pushes back at me as I push the first finger in. After a few thrusts I add a second finger, twisting and scissoring. I love seeing him writhing and wanting more, seeing him come undone under my touch. Once they glide in easily, I add a third, this time curving them to hit his prostate. Every groan is music to my ears. I don't waste too much time as I want to feel him around me. He makes no protest as I withdraw my hand and grab the lube again. I spread a layer over my cock and line up with his hole.

Fuck, it feels good when I breach him in one swift movement. Needing to fill him is like needing a drink in a drought. He cries out and I momentarily stop, but he urges me to keep going and I don't think I could go slow now even if I tried. Every thrust extracts a moan that neutralises the hurt of thirty years. Every cry says I'm sorry. Every sigh promises a better future.

I feel him tighten and his breathing hitch, and I know he's getting close to coming. The heat in my groin increases and I know I can't hold on much longer either. I pound his gland a few more times, enjoying the sound of his moans, then I start to withdraw, knowing he'll try to follow. As he does, I sink back on my heels and kneel down, wrapping my arms around his torso and pulling him back into my lap without breaking contact.

He groans and his body arches in response, but I hold him still with his back plastered across my chest. It isn't easy to move in this position but that's fine. He's so close now that I don't need to move much. I take his leaking cock in my hand, smearing the precum over it and feeling the weight of it in my hand. It only takes a few pumps before he's spilling his seed all over my fist. As he comes, his hole clenches round me, and his weight sinks down further onto me, deepening the pleasure, pulling my orgasm from me.

"*Fuuuuck.*" I'm not sure which one of us says it, it might have been simultaneous. I rest my sweaty head against his back, sated and spent.

As I feel him slump a little, I lay him down and his eyes flutter open. I brush back the sweat-soaked hair from his face and he gives me a tired but still dazzling smile.

I fetch a washcloth from the bathroom and clean him up. I lie back on the pillows and pull him into my arms.

"I'm sorry," he whispers.

"I'm sorry, too." I press a kiss to his hair.

"Dunc?" My heart squeezes at the name I haven't heard in thirty years. Others have tried to call me that, but I've never allowed it. I hadn't realised until now that I'd been reserving it just for him. I hold him a little tighter.

"Mmmm?"

"Are we going to be alright?"

My throat constricts, and I try to keep it together. He sounds so raw and vulnerable in a way that I've never heard before. We've a long way to go and a lot of ground to make up, but I truly hope so. I'm going to give it my best shot.

"We're going to be fine," I reassure him, and watch while he falls asleep.

CHAPTER 25

$\mathcal{H}$arlen

I STRETCH LANGUIDLY, awareness entering my body.

I'm not in my own bed, which means . . .

So last night *did* happen. I remember driving to Duncan's, standing outside, the coffee.

The memories seep back and I can't help a smile spreading. I feel good, my body feels *really* good . . . well, a little sore, but definitely in a nice way. I wonder if the marks are still visible. I can't see them myself, as they're mostly on my back. Thinking of Duncan leads me to notice that he's not here. That concerns me. Where is he? Did I make him uncomfortable last night?

My concern rises, and I start worrying. I'm about to climb out of bed to look for my clothes when he appears in the doorway. He's in sweatpants again, looking damn sexy. He's carrying a tray containing two mugs of coffee and a plate of toast.

"Hey," he says, smiling. "I brought breakfast." He heads to the dresser to put the tray down on it, then turns to face me.

"I . . ." I don't know how this goes. I haven't spent the whole night with someone in a very long time. I'm really rusty at this sort of stuff. I usually bail when something difficult arises. I cringe slightly when I remember I tried to run last night, and I get a warm glow when I also remember what happened after. But I realise at that moment that I've bailed all my life, every time things got too hard. I fled to Larchdown when I couldn't stand seeing Duncan happy, but before that, I hadn't told him I loved him. In a way, I'd bailed on that, too. I'd accused him of being the one that left, but that wasn't true. It was me. It's always been me. I force myself to stay calm. I want to do this. I want to stop running.

"Thank you." It's not much, but it's a start.

Thankfully, Duncan is willing to fill in the blanks for me. He hands me a coffee and I accept the steaming mug. He holds out the plate of toast and I take a piece.

"Now, we're going to have some breakfast, a shower, and then we need to talk."

Luckily, I have a mouthful of toast so I can't speak, but I nod, trying not to let the dread of what he wants to talk about overwhelm me.

SITTING at the dining room table opposite each other seems formal, and it makes me a little uncomfortable. Though I'm not sure anywhere would make me feel more at ease at this point. I try to gather my thoughts. I'd tried that in the shower, but my brain is pretty scrambled and on a loop of . . . *I think I've messed up, I'm sorry, please forgive me and give me a chance.* I work up to saying just that when Duncan starts.

"When I came here, it was like I didn't know you. I couldn't see the Harlen I knew—or thought I knew. I hated that someone had done this to you and I was angry. I didn't know that it was me. I'm also sorry for taking off again without telling you. I know I can't change the past. I'm sorry for that, but I would like to have a future with you. Can you forgive me or, at the very least, no longer hate me?"

I blink at him for a few seconds. He's seeking my forgiveness when all I've done is push him away. He deserves so much better than me.

"I don't hate you, not really. It just became easier to focus my hate on you instead of on myself. It became a coping mechanism. I thought I was safe. I was sure I'd never see you again. It was my way of dealing with it. You coming here knocked that out of kilter, and I didn't know who to hate anymore, so I lashed out. But I've never stopped loving you. I never stopped hoping, deep down, that you would come back, and I dreamed of that day.

"When my dream came true, I couldn't believe it, and although it was something I'd spent half a lifetime wanting, I pushed it away. My heart still bears the scars from that night. I don't think I could go through that again."

I stop for breath, surprised at my own admission, and he reaches out, taking my hand across the table. He gently strokes his thumb across the back. I choke back a sob at the gesture, but it's soothing. I focus on our hands and am able to carry on.

"Larchdown is my safe place, my haven. A little corner of the world where I can be me. A broken me, yes, but I'm accepted here and people care for me without being intrusive. When you waltzed in, I wanted to protect what I'd built, so I pushed you away, even though every fibre of my being wanted the opposite. Sometimes I couldn't help it, and was drawn to you like a moth to a flame. Please forgive me. I'm trying to do better."

I'm done. I can't say anything more right now, though there are still some secrets I can't tell him just yet. I'm drained and just feel numb. I can't believe that he would still want me after my explanation of why and how much of an arsehole I've been. After a few seconds, he gives my hand a little squeeze and my heart sparks back to life.

"I tried to find you."

"When?" I'm confused by what he's saying.

"Before I left for Australia. I had a relationship when I split with Gloria. Peter. He was quite a bit older than me and he was really kind, but we didn't really have much chemistry together. I'd kept in touch with Stuart and Ken from uni and they said you were with someone—Steve?"

"When was this?" My heart starts beating faster. What does this mean? He reels off the year and the month. I sit back and look at him, blinking, trying to stop my mind whirling at the revelation.

"We broke up about a month after," I say, my mouth dry.

"Why? What happened?" he asks, and I give him the truth, my voice cracking around each of the words.

"He wasn't you."

He draws in a sharp breath. "Fuck Harlen. I'm so sorry."

I shrug, trying to look much calmer than I feel. "It was a long time ago." It was, and now that I have Duncan in front of me I don't want to dwell on my past relationships, but I'm still curious about why he bothered to look for me. "Why did you try to find me?"

"I'm not wholly sure. If you'd asked me at the time, I would have probably said it was because I was lonely and I missed your friendship. But now, I think there was something deeper going on; that I felt drawn to find you."

"If things had been different, would you have stayed?"

"I might have, but I really had no reason to stay after that. I couldn't see my children and that was the hardest thing I've ever had to do. I had to move to the other side of the world and throw myself into setting up my business just to get through the day."

I can't imagine what that would have been like and how hard it must have been, and I feel shitty that my problems weren't half as bad. I've been a complete arsehole, and he's the one asking me for a second chance. I feel like some sort of low-life scum. But instead of running away, and hiding and brooding like I feel like doing, I want to try to understand.

"Tell me about being a father."

Though the sadness is still etched on his face, two pinpricks of light blaze in his eyes as he recounts how wonderful it felt to hold his children for the first time. How he'd watched them grow, their first words, taking their first steps. Their birthdays, Christmases, the first day at school.

I haven't entertained the thought of ever having children. It just wasn't on the cards for me. But he made it sound so magical that I feel a small stab of regret that it's something I'll never experience.

Then he tells me about the breakup, and the court order preventing him from having contact with them. He falters, the tears making tracks down his cheeks. This time I reach for his hand and he clasps it tightly.

"Can they really do that?" I whisper in disbelief.

"It was a long time ago, and I doubt it would be so easy now, but she—" He swallows roughly. "She convinced the court I was some sort of pervert because I lived with another man. She told them she feared for their safety. From their own father." He spits the last words and I can't stand seeing him like this. I move round to his side of the table and draw him close, holding him against me. I had no idea he had been through that. Whatever Keith said hadn't prepared me for the horror of knowing what he'd experienced. He leans into me and I close my arms around him. He doesn't say anything for a minute and then takes a few deep breaths.

He continues with the story of how, when Isabel was eighteen, she'd sought him out. How he'd sent her money for her airfare and how happy he'd been. That she'd made a wonderful life out in Australia, had met and married Gavin who works for him, and that they have two children of their own.

"Grandchildren are really the next best thing." He gives me a slightly cheeky smile. "Maybe even better, as I can indulge them to my heart's content."

"Will you miss them, being here?"

"Absolutely. But I missed so much of Jackson growing up, and I want to spend time getting to know him now. I'll visit them a few times a year."

He looks at me, and I see hope replacing the sadness.

"Next time I go back, will you come with me?"

I can't believe he just asked me that; it means so much to feel included.

"I'd love to. I'd love to meet the rest of your family."

He puts his arms round me and I hear him whisper, "They could be your family, too."

CHAPTER 26

arlen

I GLANCE around at the others in the room. The Band of Misfits, as we call ourselves. I have to make sure everyone is here, that no one's missing. An empty chair could mean many things, but it could also mean that one of us didn't make it. Didn't get through that particular day. I breathe a sigh of relief that all is well and wait for Ray to start the session.

We're all from diverse backgrounds, of all ages, and do a variety of jobs. Susan and Bob work somewhere in the corporate world, Edward and Hannah are in academia, Jess is a young stay-at-home mum, and Gareth works in a supermarket. Including me, there are seven of us. There used to be eight, but I don't dwell on that as Ray gains our attention.

We all have one thing in common; we all struggle with depression in different ways and I've found the support of the group very helpful. Sometimes seeing your problems through someone else's eyes can help gain an alternative perspective.

Each of us is called upon in turn, to introduce ourselves and tell the group what problems we've had or how we've been managing since the previous session.

I remember my first session, around five years ago. I'd been battling for a long while, and it was my doctor who suggested therapy. It had been difficult sharing anything of myself. That first time and several weeks afterwards were the hardest, and sometimes it's still difficult. It isn't usually something specific that I can pinpoint as a problem; it doesn't work like that. If it did, we might be able to combat our demons more easily. But Ray is patient and very good at his job. I was in an extremely low place when I started, but things have generally evened out, with just a few ups and down over time. It was supposed to have been a twelve-week program, but here we are years later, the same crew—well, almost. The funding ran out, but we all agreed to keep paying for Ray's time between us.

The last time I was here was just before I met Duncan in Oxford and we ended up having lunch. I'd told the group about him in a few earlier sessions, and in the one that morning they'd helped me see things from a wider angle. If I hadn't just come from a session, I'm not sure I would have said yes when he surprised me on the street. It was Bob's voice running through my head saying, *"why don't you just give him a chance?"* that had prompted me to do it. I guess I have the group to thank for a lot since then.

"Harlen. Do you want to share?" Ray's voice disturbs my reverie, and I mentally admonish myself for not paying attention when the others were speaking. I scramble to regain my composure.

"Hi, I'm Harlen, and I got laid." Fuck, I hadn't meant to say that!

Of course, I receive a chorus of whoops and cheers, and I blush a little.

"Well." Ray takes a breath. "It sounds like there have been

some positive developments. Do you want to share any more?"

A few more cheers and eager yeses, and while of course I'm not going to give them any details, I can't stop the grin on my face. I hear a contented sigh, and Hannah has a dreamy look on her face.

"I, well, yeah, it was great." I seem to have lost my power of speech, and the group erupts again.

Ray waits patiently for quiet, and asks.

"And how do you feel now?"

I take a minute before answering.

"He's a good person—a very good person—and I've realised that a lot of what I hated him for was my own cowardice. When he came back, I didn't give him a chance to explain. I didn't see he had his own story to tell. I was so wrapped up in my own hurt."

"What do you want to see in your future?" Ray prompts.

"That we can be together." I twist my fingers in my lap. I hear a few whispers from the group, and I love them for their support.

"What would your first step to that future be?" I like how Ray will always encourage you to have an action to take away from the meeting. I shrug. I'm rubbish at this sort of thing. Luckily, the group is happy to make suggestions. I hear a few, and whilst some of them are helpful, some of them are rather lewd, which gains a laugh.

"Do any of these help?"

"I suppose I could ask him to dinner." It's something I could manage.

"Are you happy with that action, though? You can always change it if you wish." Ray checks in with me.

"I can do it." I catch Hannah's eye, and she has her hands clasped under her chin and is smiling at me.

"So happy for you," she whispers, and I give her a smile back. I never thought she was a romantic.

"Thank you, Harlen." Ray turns to Bob next.

After the session, I catch Ray before we all leave.

"Ray, we should do something."

He regards me for a few seconds.

"What do you suggest?"

"I don't know, but we should get together somehow."

"You know the rules; we don't socialise outside of these meetings." I look for reproof in his voice but find none. It is frowned upon if we mix outside of the group, but I already knew Jon before we started attending the sessions.

"But we can't just do nothing. He was my friend." I can hear the desperation in my voice.

The next meeting marks a year since we lost our eighth member, Jon. He couldn't take it anymore and took his own life. I feel bad that I hadn't been able to help him enough to prevent it. We all took it badly, Ray included. I think we should honour his memory, and as a tribute to the struggles we all face I'd been trying for the last few sessions to get Ray to agree to doing something.

He sighs and nods as if thinking.

"I don't want to take away from anyone who wants support next session, but if the others are agreeable, we can extend the meeting and hold our own tribute here to him."

"Thank you. I think that would be good." It'll be sad, but I don't want to let us forget him.

Ray gives my shoulder a squeeze before heading over to the rest of the group to check that it would be alright with them.

I was going to have lunch at the café before heading back to Larchdown, but instead I go to buy some supplies. I know exactly what I'm going to cook for Duncan.

I'm pleased that we're doing something as a group. I also know there will be another memorial that day at the café. That was where I'd met Jon; he'd worked there, and he'd been Marcy's brother, too.

CHAPTER 27

 uncan

I CAN'T BELIEVE how nervous I feel as I park my car in front of Harlen's cabin. It's ridiculous, and yet here I am feeling like I'm on a first date. I suppose it really is a first date. It doesn't matter that he's my oldest friend or that we've had amazing sex. It doesn't matter that he's seen me cry. I've never actually been on a *date* date with him, and here he is inviting me to dinner—therefore a date.

It's been a couple of days since I opened up and shared my story. I hadn't wanted to. I'd put the past behind me a long time ago. I got through that pain with hard work, as well as yoga and meditation. I can't help but spare a small smile at the memory of Rob, a certain yoga instructor I'd met in Sydney. Our relationship was brief, but oh boy, did he teach me a thing or two. A strong core and flexibility can lead to a great sex life. At that thought, my nerves start dissipating. The night with Harlen was what we'd both needed to release the tension, but it had been frantic and needy. I want to spend time getting to know his body and lavishing attention on every inch of it. I want to make up for lost time. I get out of the car quickly, before I can become even more aroused at the thought of having Harlen naked under me. It wouldn't be good form to turn up on his doorstep with a raging erection. Definitely not. Ah, that's too bad then. I adjust myself in my jeans as I walk the short distance to the cabin, hoping it'll go away. But when Harlen opens the door and smiles at me, I know that it isn't going to comply with my wishes. Though he's smiling, his eyes look a little wary and unsure. I know this will be the first awkward moment, and I've noticed he doesn't seem to deal with those very well, so I make sure he understands exactly how I feel.

I move close and place a hand on the back of his neck. I ghost a soft kiss across his lips and say, "I've missed you."

The words are true. I haven't seen him for a couple of days and although I've had plenty to keep me busy, every spare thought has been turned his way.

This time the smile reaches his eyes, and he looks so goddamn sexy. I wonder if it would be impolite to skip the meal and take him to bed now instead.

"Good to see you, Dunc." Harlen shows more restraint than me and pulls back out of my arms. "Come in. Dinner will be just a few minutes."

A quick glance confirms the thought that if the bulge in his jeans is anything to go by, I'm affecting him as much as he is me, and I suppress a chuckle.

I follow him to the kitchen area.

"That smells delicious." He stirs something in a large cast-iron pan on his stove. It smells spicy, but not hot.

"It's butter chicken. It's been a while since I've made it, but it's not difficult."

"I can't wait to try it. Can I do anything to help?"

"You can grab a drink; there's some beer in the fridge."

I open the door and am greeted with a selection.

"Do you want one?" I ask him.

"Yeah, a zero, please."

I grab two and head back to open them. He frowns when he spots I have one as well.

"You don't have to do that. You can have what you want."

"I know, but this is what I want." I see a dark look flash across his face, but it doesn't go any further. A week ago I would have got a snarly remark, but I can see he's fighting it back. I don't want to ignore it and change the subject, though. We need to have the difficult conversations too.

"Have you given up drinking for good?"

"I don't know, probably not." He shrugs, "It'll give me something to fall back on when I realise this is all a dream."

Fuuuccckk!

Is he still feeling that insecure?

That would explain his wariness when I'd arrived. Had he thought I wouldn't turn up? I know I messed up going back to Sydney the way I did. And whilst I hadn't thought we could undo thirty years of hurtful feelings that easily, I didn't expect him to throw it out there like this.

It hurts to know he still thinks that. I know I deserve some of it, but somehow I don't think he truly does believe it, and I'm really not one to start arguments. If he lashes out like that, then he is still hurting, and I want to erase that more than anything.

I cross the short distance between us and take him by the shoulders.

"Do you really think that?"

He looks at me for a second. "I'm trying not to, I really am." Then his shoulders slump and he drops his head. "I'm sorry. I told you I was messed up. Here you are, all I ever wanted, and I

125

can't even enjoy it. I have to open my big mouth and fuck it up."

I place my hand under his chin and raise his head so he has to look at me.

"Tell me what you fear the most?"

He swallows before answering. "That you'll realise you don't want me after all, and the dream I had, the hope I've held on to for so long, was all for nothing." He gives a wry smile. "The one thing about never having your dreams come true is, they can't turn to dust in your hands."

I get that, I really do, but we can't move on until he gets over this.

"There are no absolutes in this world, darling. I can't promise what the future will bring. But I know you, and I know I want to give us the best shot we can. I think we're going to be great together. I was given some good advice recently which told me that if it was worth it, I needed to grab it with both hands. I've done that. If you truly think we're worth it, then I need you to do the same. Can you let go of the handrail and join me in the deep end?"

"Sink or swim?" He still looks sad, but he doesn't look warily defensive any more.

"I'll have you know I'm an excellent swimmer," I reply, and that gets me the beginnings of a smile.

"I'm sorry. I really am Dunc. There's no reason for me to feel this way, but sometimes I just can't help it." Something in his words makes me realise that there's more to this than I first thought. I don't know what that is right now, but this is not the time to dig deeper. I shelve that thought for later and concentrate on how he's feeling now. I pull him towards me and into a hug. He only slightly resists before he submits and lets me hold him.

"No more sorrys, okay?" I say soothingly. "We're going to be fine."

I feel him nod against my chest and I release him slowly.

"Now, I don't know about you but I'm starving, and if I have to wait any longer for food, then I might just have to feed myself." I head to the stove and give the food a stir. That does the trick, and I'm batted off and told to sit down at the table.

I readily comply, and before long he places the chicken, a bowl of rice, and a salad on the table.

"Help yourself." He gestures to the food, and I waste no time in tucking in because I meant it when I said I was starving.

I keep topics on easy subjects, mostly asking him about the work he's got lined up, especially at Larchdown House, and what his work pattern is throughout the year. He visibly relaxes throughout the meal, and I'm pleased that he seems better.

"Have you had enough?" he asks, as I finish my food and sit back.

"That was really good. I don't think I've ever had that before."

"I got the recipe from a friend." He gives a wistful look, as if recalling a bittersweet memory.

"Well, tell them thank you," I say.

"I can't," he says bluntly, but doesn't elaborate. Then he gives me a grin. "Do you have room for dessert?"

"What is it?"

He gives me a look I *do* recognise, and I know exactly what he's about to say, so I say it at the same time.

"Tiramisu!"

He throws his head back, and there it is—the laugh I've been waiting for. The one I remember and love so much.

His eyes are shining as he fetches the dessert. Nowadays, tiramisu is really commonplace, but thirty years ago it was considered pretty exotic, especially for students on a meagre budget. We used to eat it when we could afford it, pretending we were posh people who ate it every day. We would affect fake posh accents and call each other "dear." It was stupid and juvenile, but it was fun. That he remembers and wants to recreate that part of our past means more to me than any words.

I feel a warmth blooming through my chest and settling in my bones, along with the knowledge that I will spend the rest of my days making up for lost time.

"Why thank you, *my dear*," I say, as he hands me a bowl. I devour my dessert in a few spoonfuls. "That was absolutely delightful."

"I'm glad you found it a pleasurable experience." He chuckles, and the sound of it sparks my arousal.

"I can think of many more pleasurable experiences I could have with you," I reply, my voice thick with desire.

His eyes swirl as he looks at me. "Yes, please."

CHAPTER 28

arlen

The words are barely out of my mouth before Duncan is round to my side of the table and offering me a hand up. I'd barely seen him move. He leans close to my ear, and with a voice so rich and dark it goes straight to my groin he whispers, "Well, since you asked so nicely."

With my hand still in his, he leads me up the wooden staircase to my bedroom, which is nestled in the roof space of my cabin. I can see him run his architect's eye round it and he smiles at me.

"This is gorgeous." His praise makes me blush for some reason, but I'm pleased he likes it. I made all the furniture myself, but I can see his attention is now riveted on the headboard. So much so that he drops my hand and goes over to it and runs his fingers over the carving. It's a woodland scene, complete with trees, creatures, and birds. It reminds me of the view across the valley.

"This is incredible," he says, his voice sounding reverent. "Did you make this?" He turns to me, and although I'm used to people saying nice things about my work, it seems more special from him, and I suddenly feel a bit self-conscious under his praise.

"I made it all." I shrug, trying to play it down, but he isn't buying it. Sitting on the side of my bed, he motions with his hands for me to come closer. I stand in front of him and he looks up at me.

"I knew you were talented, but this . . ." He gestures to the headboard. "This is exquisite. Do you know how much you could sell something like that for?"

I have no interest in making them for other people. I don't want entitled, too-wealthy clients who change their minds on a whim or who put pressure on me to make things faster. I don't need the money. I have enough to live on and that's fine by me.

"It's not for sale," is my blunt reply. Duncan catches my hands and holds them in front of him.

"These are talented tools." He gives them a squeeze. "But I'm more interested in the brain behind them."

He stands and leans forward to press a kiss to my lips. It's soft at first, but then it deepens and I'm with him. One moment following and the other leading. His tongue swirls with mine. There's no clashing, no fighting for dominance or possession. Just a dance of equals, a symphony that feels so right in my bones that my stomach swoops and my knees become weak. I don't want it to end. I'm floating on a cloud, suspended in a perfect summer sky, but I'm also running out of air. Even the ending is like a gentle coda, a soft withdrawal, with a couple of postscript touches that make my lips tingle. With the final graze of his lips across mine, Duncan rests his forehead against mine, as breathless as I am, trying to draw air into his lungs. As I look into his brown eyes, I feel the widest smile I can ever remember making, spread across my face.

"Worth waiting thirty years for?" he asks, mirroring my grin.

"Just don't make me wait thirty more years for another like that," I reply, chuckling.

"I promise." He gives a breathy laugh back at me.

I've recovered my breath a little and my legs now feel a bit stronger, so I stand up straighter. My knees crack, and Ducan chuckles as I grimace. I don't really need a reminder of how old I am right at this moment.

"You should try yoga," he suggests.

"What, naked yoga?" I tease, and he smirks. "Wait, have you done naked yoga? You have, haven't you?"

The light dances in his eyes and the thought of him making poses in the buff is too much. I start unbuttoning his shirt, desperate to get my hands on him. This time, unlike the frantic energy of a few days ago, I take the time to run my hands over his body as I strip him of his shirt. He's lean but not ripped, which I like. His skin is tanned—must be all that outdoor Aussie living. I trail my fingers through the dusting of hair he has, and I feel him shiver at my touch.

He places a hand on the nape of my neck and pulls me forward into another kiss, as if our mouths have been apart too long. When he starts undressing me, I keep up a light touch on his skin, running my fingers up and down his arms and across his stomach, enjoying how much it distracts him as he hums into my mouth.

He unbuckles my jeans and strips them down my legs in one swift movement. I step out of them and kick them aside. He cups a hand on my arse cheek, pulling me to him. With a glint in his eye, he spins me round and pushes me down onto the bed.

"Do you have lube?" He asks casually.

"Top drawer." I gesture towards the drawers next to the bed. He retrieves it and throws it down on the bed. Then he takes his own jeans off, and lies down on his side next to me, his elbow crooked, and his head resting on his hand.

He trails a hand across my chest. "You're beautiful," he whispers.

"I'm too old for that," I protest, feeling self-conscious.

"Nonsense." He smiles at me, his hand never ceasing its movements, stroking up and down my body. He traces a finger over a scar on my abdomen.

"What caused this one?" he murmurs.

"A tree branch. It broke and speared me, but luckily it missed anything vital. It must have been around fifteen years ago."

"And this?" He pushes lightly at a dip on my arm, where the muscle had never quite recovered its shape.

"I slipped with a wood chisel. A stupid mistake."

He hums in what feels like sympathy, then he lightly touches a silvery scar that circles my inner thigh. The nerves have always been a bit different on that one. The sensation is somewhat distant, as if it's not my body, but it's also overly sensitive, as if the nerve endings are exposed on the outside of my skin. His touch sends sparks across my skin and increases my arousal. I'm finding it difficult to keep breathing.

"Mmmm, what was this?" His voice is like honey.

"Rope burn," I manage to get out. I catch my breath. "Dunc, what are you doing?"

"Mapping your body. Every mark, every scar, is an experience that I wasn't there for. I'm trying to catch up, to learn your history. I want to know every one of them."

I don't know what I've done to deserve this man. I'm not sure I could love him more than I do, and yet he continues to surprise me. I realise that the love I held onto for so long was just an idea—a facsimile—it was like grasping at clouds. But *this*, what I feel now, coils its way around my bones and organs and becomes symbiotic. Separating it would be akin to ripping out a part of me, the heart of me. I watch his fingers alight on every one of the smaller nicks and scars that are part of the job I do, and I only hope that one day I have the courage to show him the ones on the inside too.

Every thought is blown from my head as he drags his tongue across my thigh scar, and it elicits a sinful moan from me as every nerve in my body is locked on to that spot. Then he peppers kisses up my leg and licks a stripe up my groin.

"Jeez, fuck." I hiss, then his touch is gone.

He shifts and straddles me, his hands either side of my head. He claims a kiss, and I want to devour his mouth. I try to follow him as he pulls away, running open-mouthed kisses down my neck and shoulders.

I feel his lips gently close round my leaking cockhead, his tongue sliding through my precum. Somehow, his attention is more potent for its delicacy, and I nearly come straight away. As he takes me deeper into his throat, I can't resist tangling my fingers in his hair. I try to gain a bit more friction, but he resists, and the featherlight contact he maintains with his lips and tongue running up and down my shaft keeps me in a delicious agony.

I'm so lost in focussing on the torturously slow ministrations to my cock, that I almost jump off the bed when I feel a slick finger slowly tease my hole. As it circles my pucker, I want to feel it inside me, and I wriggle slightly. Duncan places his other hand on my stomach to keep me still, and I'm rewarded with him leisurely pushing one finger in. Never before have I wanted to be filled so completely and I push back, trying to get more, but he pulls his finger out. I utter a string of curses but stay still, and almost cry with relief when the finger returns. After a few seconds, he adds another finger and I sigh in contentment. My world narrows to the sensation of the languid thrusting of his fingers in my hole and my cock still encased by his mouth, his tongue rhythmically brushing over the head and across my slit.

I see stars when, with a twist, he grazes across my prostrate. Not every time, but enough to hold me in an almost catatonic state. I desperately need more, but with his hand firmly holding me so I can't move, I'm reduced to begging. I'm not ashamed of the whine that comes from me.

"Please Dunc, I need more."

He emits a low growl from around my cock and adds a third finger. It's divine, and I drift for a while, riding the swell of the building pressure. I hardly recognise my own voice this time as I wail.

"Please give it to me, all of it."

He drops his mouth down to my root and sucks deeply, pulling my soul back with him.

"Ngngnggngh."

Then he pops off, and I curse at the loss of his mouth.

"Shhh," he soothes, increasing the pace of his fingers, which are still buried deep inside me. I feel my balls lift and my abs tighten when his fingers vanish too, but this time, before I can rain a barrage of expletives at him, he plunges his dick straight into me, up to the hilt.

"Fuuccking hell!" I tense slightly at the momentary burn, and then relax with the feeling of being gloriously filled, as he settles every inch of himself inside me. He begins to roll his hips, and the leisurely pace he took with his fingers is replaced by a brisk motion. Over and over he drives into me and carries me even closer to the edge. I feel his balls slap against me, a rhythmic noise to the backdrop of our panting.

His lips connect with mine, and I clasp my hands to the back of his neck, holding him there, tasting myself in his mouth.

He keeps up the relentless pace which, with every nudge of my gland, cuts me adrift from reality.

I finally come in a crescendo of stars, and as the waves of my orgasm wash over me, I feel him spill deep inside of me. My universe explodes, and I become weightless atoms floating in the ether.

uncan

"Do you normally have morning wood, or are you just pleased to see me?"

I chuckle at the corny line, but press myself further against Harlen's arse. Waking up with him in my arms is turning out to be one of my favourite things, especially if I'm spooned into him, and my cock wants to get in on it, too.

He'd been too blissed out last night to notice when I'd cleaned us up and then climbed into bed and curled myself around him. I haven't slept so deeply in a long while and I feel wonderfully refreshed . . . and also horny.

"Mmmm." I wriggle to get a little more friction, but instead, Harlen pulls away and turns over to face me.

"I was enjoying that!" I'm too old to pout, but I try it anyway. It fails.

Harlen gives me an amused look. "Please never do that again. You look like a constipated orangutan."

"*Oooft*, moodkiller."

"So was your look." He grins, pushing me onto my back and sitting astride my legs. He fists my cock.

"That's better." I smile and relax as he reaches for the lube. I was going to close my eyes and lose myself to his touch, but the sight of him bringing himself off at the same time is way too hot to miss. I watch as he throws his head back, his throat exposed, which almost demands to have my lips and my teeth on it. I struggle to resist the urge to flip him and fuck him. Instead, I content myself with the memory of how sensitive he was to my touch last night and how undone he became under me. With those thoughts in my head—Harlen's hand pumping my cock and his own while he stretches above me—it takes very little time before I'm covering my own chest with spurts of cum. Harlen's own release coming a few seconds later.

"Good Morning," he says, and leans down to press a kiss to my lips.

"I'd say so," I reply. I look down at the cooling mess on my torso. "Shower?"

"You go ahead, I'll fix some coffee." He climbs off me and reaches for some sweats.

"You could join me," I suggest. And he turns, hopping with one leg in his sweatpants.

"I didn't anticipate showering with company when I built this house, so there isn't room for us both." He gives a rueful little smile which looks adorable. I mentally thank myself that I'd thought about that when designing the valley house. My thoughts stray to the sinful things I could do to Harlen in the shower room there, as I head to the *very* compact shower cubicle Harlen had wedged into his cabin house. In reality, I probably don't have time to linger in the shower anyway. I need to get up to the site as work starts today. A look at my watch while getting dressed confirms that I only have an hour before I need to be on site. Had I really slept so long? The thought pleases me greatly and I'm looking forward to repeating it—and the night before—as soon as possible.

I descend to the living area to the smell of coffee and toast, which has to be one of the greatest scent combinations in the universe.

Harlen is at the counter spreading butter on toast. I wrap my arms round him from behind and nuzzle a kiss into his neck. When I lift my face, he's holding out a piece of toast over his shoulder, and I instinctively open my mouth and take it. I release one hand, as I need to hold the toast to take a bite, but then I drop a buttery kiss on his neck before letting go completely. The easy domesticity and feeling of rightness of this overwhelms me a little, and I turn away to compose myself before reaching for the coffee Harlen hands out.

"Everything ok?" he asks, frowning a little.

"Perfect," I answer. Because it is. I take a swig of coffee, preparing myself to ask the next question. "Do you feel ready to tell people about us?"

Harlen puts down his coffee and runs his hand over his jaw. He's at least giving the question some consideration.

"I think so. What do you suggest?"

"Well, I'd like to tell Jackson first if that would be alright?"

He nods.

"Then we can go from there."

"Okay," he agrees, but I can see he isn't totally comfortable.

"I'm going to the house tonight. Jackson invited me to dinner, to celebrate work starting on my place."

"Shit, is that today? Sorry, I forgot." He looks apologetic.

"It's fine," I reassure him. "I haven't said much about it recently, but I could do with your help in a couple of days if you're free, just to double check on the site plan and the trees we are keeping." The "we" slips out unbidden. Although I think of us in relation to my house, I know I can't broach that with him yet, but if he notices, he doesn't say anything.

"I can be there," he confirms.

"Great, thanks. And will you come with me tonight?"

"To dinner?" He suddenly looks a little unsure.

"Yes. It'll be fine, I promise." I close the gap between us and slowly rub my hands up and down his upper arms, hoping to reassure him. He agrees, and I draw him into a hug, thankful that he said yes. I place a kiss on his lips.

"Now I have to go."

Kiss

"I really have to go."

Kiss

"I'm going to be late."

This time, I press him up against the counter and kiss him properly. I could spend all day with his tongue halfway down my throat. With a groan, I slowly stop.

"That will have to do until later."

He cocks an eyebrow at me, and it unravels my resolve. I need another taste of him and grab him again for another long kiss. This time I don't stop until I need to draw breath.

"See what you've done to me?" I place Harlen's hand on my crotch, where he can clearly feel how hard I am.

"You think you're the only one?" He quirks a smile at me, and I look down to where I can see his tented sweatpants. It's my turn to look at him with an apology in my eyes.

"Go, you'll be late." He places a hand on my chest. "I'll be thinking of you while I'm in the shower."

I force myself to turn away with a loud groan. That image does nothing to help deal with my boner, quite the opposite, but I'm out of time. I grab my keys and give him one last look.

"Pick you up at seven?" I take in his shining eyes, his lips bruised from my kisses, and his visible arousal. "Scrub that. I'll be here at six."

He laughs, and my heart tightens around the sound. I want to make him laugh like that every day.

. . .

I MAKE it to the site a few minutes late and apologise to Holly, but she brushes it off as not a big deal. I think she's too excited to get this started to be annoyed with me. Today is just setting up the access to get the delivery vehicles to the site. There's no roadway in place as it's in the woods, and this has to be constructed first. We go through the details of how this will happen now that we're onsite, and everything is exactly as she'd planned it out. I'm reassured by her confidence. She goes through the next few stages, and I tell her that Harlen will be here in two days. I don't want any trees removed until he confirms them himself. She agrees and seems pleased to be able to ask some questions.

As everything seems to be in hand, I leave her to it with the promise that I'll check in daily until things are properly underway. I head back to the cottage to catch up with some work. There are a few emails that require responses and a reminder about a meeting with a new client tomorrow.

I nearly miss the email from Gavin. I answer it anyway, even though it's night-time over there. I curse myself, had I not stayed the night with Harlen, I would have been able to check my emails this morning before Gavin finished for the day. Though if it had been urgent, he could have called me, so I don't feel too bad about it. I make a note to catch up with him and Isabel properly tomorrow. No doubt she'll be wanting the latest news about Harlen and, whilst there is news, she will be getting the heavily censored version. I grab some lunch and then work for the rest of the afternoon.

"READY?" I ask Harlen, as I stop the car in front of Larchdown House.

"I think so." He nods, seeming to convince himself. "No, I'm definitely ready."

"It'll be fine." I lean over to claim a kiss. Not that I haven't spent the last hour kissing him. Except for the time my mouth was wrapped around his cock, of course. I certainly didn't waste the time we had. We're almost late, as I just couldn't seem to break off from him again. Not that he wasn't making it difficult for me as well. He's like a drug I can't get enough of. I feel the need to keep the very essence of him topped up in my soul.

We climb out of the car. I feel excited to tell Jackson. I'd told him I was bringing someone with me to dinner but I hadn't told him any more than that.

Jackson opens the door promptly, with a ready smile on his face.

"Hi Harlen. I wasn't expecting to see you." He looks a little puzzled, and I see him glance past us to see if there was anyone else there.

I feel Harlen tense up next to me. "I can go—" he starts, but I interject.

"I thought it was important that we came together." I watch as Jackson's puzzled look deepens, and then he half-smiles.

"Together?" I feel the weight of his question.

"Yes, together."

He grins widely and ushers us into the house. "Why? How? When?" Then replaces it with another frown. "Wait, I thought you barely liked each other."

"It's a long story, but your dad and I, well, we go way back." Harlen looks more comfortable now that he seems sure of Jackson's reception.

Jackson grins. "I want to know it all, but first, can we tell Luca?"

"Of course," I reply, eager to see Luca's reaction. Jackson

disappears for a few minutes, and I step closer to Harlen and catch his hand.

"Still alright?"

"Yes, I'm more than good. This is a relief, isn't it? To tell someone?"

"It is. Though I'd like to shout it from the rooftops."

He grimaces at me. "Can we just stick to telling a few friends for now?"

"Absolutely." I squeeze his hand and keep hold of it when Jackson comes back with Luca in tow.

"Hi Dad, hi Harlen. Jackson said you had some amazing news." He looks from me to Harlen and back again. Harlen lifts our hands, which are still connected.

"Duncan and I knew each other at uni, but let's just say we've . . . reconnected." He smiles at me as he says it, and a warm feeling blooms across my chest.

"Oh. My. God! That's fantastic!" Luca exclaims loudly, and then we're enveloped in hugs from Jackson and Luca. They're both repeating how wonderful it is, how they're so pleased for me and Harlen, how they almost thought him part of the family already and were excited to welcome him officially.

Eventually, they shoo us into the dining room and bustle off to the kitchen to finish dinner. I turn to Harlen and see tears running down his face.

"Hey darling, what is it?" I cup his face with my hands and wipe the tears away with my thumbs.

"It's . . ." I see him swallow. "I just didn't expect that much. They're great, aren't they? Your son is wonderful."

"Not my doing, but yes, he is. They both are." I plant a kiss on each of his cheeks and then one on his lips.

"Thank you. And Jackson is more like you than you give yourself credit for." He gives me a small smile, and there is nothing I wouldn't do to keep him smiling forever.

We're bombarded with questions throughout dinner. A few

about how we found each other again, but mostly about what we were like at uni. I love seeing Harlen relax and join in. He unwinds enough to tell some embarrassing stories about me.

As we're leaving, Jackson stops me and asks if he could have Isabel's contact details. I'm delighted that he wants to get in touch with his sister. I know she'll be pleased, and she's already said she'd like to see him again. I feel lucky to be rebuilding my family, and that Harlen is a part of it.

CHAPTER 30

$\mathcal{H}$arlen

MY HEART SKIPS a beat when I see Duncan waiting for me at the tower. I can't believe he turned up. But then, why wouldn't he? He doesn't know what I'm going to show him yet. After today, it might be very different.

Today I'm going to show him me—the real me, not the guy he remembers from years ago. As much as I would like to be that person, I'm not him anymore.

He smiles broadly as I approach. I don't think I'll ever tire of seeing that smile. Although his face now shows his age, he looks bloody good for it. His smile is still the same as it's always been, the same sunshine which has been a lodestar for me. My breath hitches as I remember how I'd thought I'd never see it again, and try not to think that I might not if this goes wrong. I force myself to take a few deep breaths to try to calm my nerves.

I have to believe in myself and believe in him. I've just

talked this through in my therapy session, and the others were very supportive. They assured me it would all be okay. But then, they only have the snippets of Duncan that I feed them. I keep the special moments to myself.

"Hey beautiful." He hugs me and gives me a kiss, and everything seems alright with the world.

"Hi. I'm glad you came."

"Why wouldn't I have come?" He frowns at me, so I catch his hand and start walking, suddenly needing to get it over and done with.

"Is everything alright?" he asks, and I can hear the worry in his voice.

"No questions." I glance at him. "Please, no questions for now."

"Okay." He still sounds worried, but allows himself to be pulled along.

Luckily, the cemetery isn't far, and it doesn't take long to walk there. We enter through the black, ornate, wrought-iron gates and I steer him down the paths. In this part, the graves are old, and some of the headstones stand at odd angles, slumped with time and neglect. Most of them are weathered and the inscriptions are no longer legible. Others are covered with moss and lichen. Occasionally, there are also well-tended graves, which families keep well maintained so loved ones still have somewhere to remember. It makes me sad to think of the ones for people who have faded from memory or no longer have someone to mourn them.

We work our way over to the section of more recent burials, and eventually I pull him to a stop in front of one. He looks at the grave and then at me. Concern is etched on his face, along with questions that I can see bubbling up. But he keeps them locked in. I'm thankful for that as I need to think clearly for this bit.

"This is Jon. He was Marcy's brother. You know, Marcy from the café?"

He gives a quick nod, and I continue.

"But he was also my friend. A good friend for a number of years. I met him at the café. He worked for Marcy, usually in the gardens and doing odd jobs. Today is the anniversary of his death." I choke over the last words, unable to go on for a minute.

"I'm sorry for your loss." Duncan gives my hand a squeeze, and I want him to know everything.

"You don't understand. It could have been me. It could have been any of us. All it takes is one bad day. One time, when hope seems impossible. One day, when it all gets too much and you can't see a way out of the abyss. I wish I had known how bad it was for him at that time, but I was busy. When we're at the bottom of the well, we don't think to ask for help climbing out. I didn't know until it was too late."

I pause for a minute, my eyes stinging with the tears threatening to spill over, but I want to hold it together. I need to finish this.

"It was Marcy who found him, hanging from the garage rafters. She blames herself, that she got delayed at work, but that day it was me she was talking to. We were discussing plans for a birthday celebration, for him, for the following week. So it's my fault, too."

I can't hold back any longer. The guilt runs in rivulets down my face. Duncan draws me into a hug and I let him, needing the physical touch for a minute. But I'm not finished yet, and I still need him to see me, who I really am. I push back and put a hand on his chest to prevent him from pulling me to him again. Because if he does, I don't think I'll be able to stop myself from never leaving the comfort of his arms again.

"I said it could have been me," I say, my voice barely more than a whisper. "I knew Jon from somewhere else as well. He was a member of the same group as me. We meet every couple of weeks. It's a therapy group. We're all different, but we're all fighting our own demons."

I stop and turn my head away, unable to look at him. It will kill me to see the disgust and rejection I've convinced myself I would find there. Or pity. I don't want that either.

I feel hands on either side of my face, gently easing it back round. I close my eyes.

"Thank you for telling me this. I understand it must have been hard for you." His voice sounds raw, and I allow myself to take a peek at him. Is he crying, too?

"I have no idea what it must have been like, what it feels like, but trust me when I say I'm here for you. I will always be here for you, if you'll let me."

Relief floods through me, and this time I seek his embrace. I don't know how long we stand there wrapped in each other's arms, but eventually I pull back and wipe my eyes with the back of my hand. I give him a watery smile.

"I was sure you'd never want to see me again," I say, and watch his features crease into a frown.

"I'm so sorry that I've ever caused you to think that about me. That you couldn't trust me. But I love you, Harlen. I don't want to be anywhere but by your side, whatever you're facing." He brushes my hair away from my damp cheeks.

"You love me?" I blurt out.

"I do. With everything I have in me." He kisses me and gives me one of his beautiful, tender smiles.

"But all I've done is try to push you away."

"It doesn't work like that, my love. I don't think I could stay away if I tried. I didn't recognise that there was a part of me that had been missing, until I saw you again." He reaches for my hand and holds it to his chest, to his heart. "I'm not going to dwell on lost time, but I love you, and I want us to tread this journey together—if you'll have me."

"I've waited half a lifetime to hear you say that." I try not to cry again as he lifts my hand to his lips and kisses my knuckles. Then he interlaces our fingers and we continue walking.

"There's a small gathering at the café today, in Jon's memory. Would you come with me?" I ask after a couple of minutes, when I feel able to speak normally again.

"I'd love to. It would be an honour."

We leave the cemetery and head towards the café.

"Can I ask some questions now?" he asks tentatively.

"Yes, if you want to." I expect something about the sessions or something technical, but instead he surprises me.

"Tell me about Jon? What were the things you admired most about him?"

And so I tell him as we walk to the café. I recount some of the times we shared; how sometimes he would be full of laughter, but at other times I could see it was a struggle for him. I tell how he was a loyal friend, and that he always had a kind word to say about everyone.

Duncan keeps up the questions, and I relax as we walk. We reach the café and Duncan pulls me to a stop.

"I have so much more I want to know about you, as much as you feel comfortable telling me. But I want you to promise me something."

He waits, and I slowly look up at him.

"Promise me, that if you ever feel yourself tipping over the edge, you'll try to let me know. Try to let me help you."

I notice the absence of absolutes in his request. He understands I cannot give him that, and I know in that moment that he truly sees me. I can only nod, and he gives me the softest kiss that feels more intimate and sincere than anything we've shared before.

CHAPTER 31

uncan

"We have a request," Jackson says one Friday over lunch. I've taken to joining them one day a week. Sometimes Harlen joins us as well, and I love it when he does. It makes me feel that I have my family around me, well, most of them. Harlen is with us today and he looks a lot more relaxed. Many of the shadows that had hung about him have been chased away.

It's full summer, so the gardens are open to the public on a couple of weekdays as well as the weekends. Their business is thriving and I'm happy for Jackson and Luca. It's getting a reputation outside of the region, and is attracting more visitors, too. It's good for the village as well, as more people bring customers to the other businesses in the area. Every time I go to The Arms, Darla looks busy.

"Sure, what can I help you with?" I reply, and see him look over at Luca.

"We're planning to visit Isabel, and as we don't like to leave the house empty, would you house-sit for us?"

"That's great! I'm so pleased that you and Isabel are getting on well." I *love* that Jackson wants to reconnect with his sister, and I'm sure they'll get on well. I know Isabel is going to love Luca too. "Of course I will. When are you thinking of going?"

"Not until autumn. We'll be going sometime after we close the gardens for the season."

That's a relief, as I don't think I could look after having the public onsite as well. I know they have some help, but it's a big responsibility.

"That's okay, then. I don't fancy having to watch people trample over your lawns."

"Thanks Dad," he says with a wink. "You can stay as well, Harlen."

Seeing Harlen spit out his drink is amusing, though he does look a bit flustered. Being given the run of your boyfriend's son's house as if you're a horny teenager, might have caught him by surprise, but Jackson just laughs and gives his shoulder a squeeze. He recovers enough to answer.

"I've earmarked to trim the trees on the drive in the autumn, so it would be a good time to do it then." He looks pleased that he can justify his presence here, especially when Jackson replies that it sounds like perfect timing.

I tease him about it later. I've taken the afternoon off and Harlen doesn't have any work on, so I drive us back to Lilac Cottage. We're in the kitchen making coffee.

"So then, do you think you can manage to spend a few weeks with me house-sitting, or do you need to conjure up a reason for being there?"

He looks a bit bashful.

"I felt a bit embarrassed. I know Jackson and Luca are great, but I'm still getting used to them knowing me like this. It felt better to give it a professional footing."

I move closer and bracket him in my arms, pinning him against the countertop.

"So, can I seduce the lumberjack and invite him back to my house for extra *wood* work after hours?" Whilst his mouth quirks at my words, I can see his eyes darken, and my briefs suddenly feel too tight. I lean in and plant a row of open-mouthed kisses on his jaw and neck.

"You know what they say?" I ask against his skin.

"Mmmnn."

"Practice makes perfect."

I hear a breathy chuckle. "Who needs practice?"

"Oh, I do." I move my hands to his belt buckle and undo his jeans. "There's nothing more I want to do than keep practising, over, and over."

I drop to my knees and release his cock from his boxers. Taking it into my hand, I lick a stripe up the underneath and across his cockhead, dipping my tongue into his slit for a taste of his precum. After swirling my tongue round his glans, I take all of him into my mouth. I grab his arse and pull him further in, pushing past the gag sensation. I bury my nose in the hair at the base of his cock and inhale his essence. I hum contentedly round him, hearing him groan. I slowly start moving, playing my tongue along his length. Picking up speed, I suck him in and out, slurping with pleasure, drool running down my chin.

I look up at him and I see his bliss-filled eyes, hands gripping the countertop. I wipe a finger across my chin, gathering up saliva and precum. As I tease it up his crease, he hisses.

"Fucking hell Dunc. That feels so good."

He grabs the back of my head, holding me steady while he pumps his hips, fucking my mouth. I keep humming and squelching and making all the greedy sounds I can, loving how he's using me. I trail my fingers down his taint and pull down on his balls, and feel them tighten as he shoots his load into my mouth. I take it all, enjoying the taste of him.

I stand up and he pulls me in for a kiss, swooping his tongue in to taste himself, which I find irresistibly hot.

"I think that was pretty much perfect," he gasps.

"Don't you deny me my practice," I retort, nipping at his neck. "I clearly need to be better—you're still able to stand up after all."

PART III
AUTUMN

CHAPTER 32

uncan

"What's left to do?" I ask Holly, shielding my eyes from the low autumnal afternoon sun and looking up at the house. I can't quite believe how quickly it has taken shape—it looks magnificent. It flows out of the side of the valley, and with the centre section made of glass stretching out towards the trees, it almost looks like it's floating amid the forest. The grass-covered roof is both warming and eco-friendly, and when the alpine style flowers grow in the spring, a carpet of blues and purples will blend in well.

"Just the final interior fittings. It will be another couple of weeks, three tops, providing the stone arrives on time." Holly looks for my reaction.

"Has there been a problem?" The stone is for the bathrooms. The tiles and the unit tops are being hand-cut from Turkish stone and polished.

"The company said there'd been a delay in shipping, but

they're expecting it today and will get on to cutting them straight away."

"Oh, that doesn't sound too bad then." I've learned over the months that Holly runs a really tight ship and hates any form of delay. She can usually find a workaround, and did so when the glass supplier cut the large windows the wrong way round, repurposing them for another project and having them remade within days. If she says it'll be ready in a couple of weeks or so, then I believe her. I'm looking forward to it. I have already chosen most of the furniture. I've asked Harlen to help me pick out some of the furnishings, because not only does he have great taste, but I want him to have a part in it. I'd really love for him to come and live with me here. I want to take our relationship to that level, but I'm also aware that he feels most comfortable when he's at his cabin. I know how much it means to him and I don't think he'll want to leave. I will ask him at some point, but maybe not until I've moved in.

The timing is great, as Jackson and Luca are due back from Australia by then. They've been away for just over a week and I'm enjoying looking after the old house; it has a lot of character. Now that I have a plan, I can also give up the cottage, as I know Pete already has another tenant lined up for it. I don't have much stuff there, so I can move out pretty much straight away.

I make arrangements to meet Holly the following day, as she wants to go through a couple of the final details, and then make my way back to Larchdown house.

When I get back, Harlen is tidying up some of the branches from the trees he's maintaining on the drive.

"Do you want some help?" I stop the car and ask, knowing full well that he'll refuse, considering me not suitably dressed. He'd be right; I've been meeting with clients for most of the day, so I have on a smart pair of trousers, a shirt, and a sweater. He, of course, looks gorgeously rugged in his work trousers and check shirt.

"No, I'm good. It won't take me long to finish up here. I'll be up in a bit."

I carry on and park the car. He won't be long, as the sun is setting and it'll be too dark soon.

He comes in about twenty minutes later.

I hand him a coffee, which he takes gratefully. He leans in for a kiss and I get a nose full of his delicious musk.

"See, you've got all sweaty doing that work on your own," I tease. "Now I'm going to have to get you cleaned up."

It's a ruse. I've been wanting to try out the big shower here since coming to look after the place, and I can't think of anything I'd like better than to clean him up . . . before I get him messy again.

"Mmm, I like the sound of that," he replies. "But can you hold off for a few minutes?"

"What for?" There can't possibly be anything he needs to do in the gathering dusk.

"I need to nip back home and put the batteries on charge. I still have a few things I need to finish tomorrow, but I've run out of power, so I need to get them charging overnight."

"Okay, but hurry back or I might start without you." He laughs and finishes his coffee.

While he's gone, I open my laptop and check a few work emails, pleased to see one from Gabriel Barclay-Sinclair about a contract for designing the new restaurant and spa complex at the polo club, before wandering into the kitchen to decide what we should have for dinner.

CHAPTER 33

*H*arlen

I'M as quick as I can be back at my cabin. I duck into the workshop to put the batteries on charge. I'd even used the spares today, so I switch on several chargers.

Electric tools are easier and lighter than the old petrol-driven ones I used to use, but when you've run out of power, that's it until they're charged again.

I quickly grab some clean clothes from the house and make my way back to Larchdown House. Staying there has been really good, and sharing space with Duncan has been surprisingly easy. Maybe because it's a neutral space, and we don't feel like we're crowding into each other's domain. I've been alone for so long I thought it would be more difficult, but actually, it's nice having someone there to talk to— to share things with. And let's not forget the sex. No one has ever made me feel the way Duncan does; it's like he knows every part of my body and how to make it react to his touch. Just thinking about it has me driving a little faster than I should on the country lanes to hurry back to him, but thankfully, I arrive safely.

"Dunc?" I call when I enter the house. I come into the kitchen and kick my boots off, depositing them in the utility room. I don't get an answer, so I move through the house and into the lobby.

"Dunc?" I call again, this time receiving an answer from the upper floor. I take the stairs two at a time and locate him in the bedroom we've been sharing. It's a large room that overlooks the main driveway. Duncan is dressed in a fluffy bathrobe, and something about it makes me want to rip it off him. I reach for him, but he dances away, out of my grasp.

"I want you to strip first," he says, sitting on the bed, looking relaxed.

I start taking my shirt off and he growls at me to go slower. So he wants the full show? I'm happy to oblige. I spare a glance at him and feel a thrill that I can see his eyes are glassy, and he's slowly stroking himself under his robe. That makes me hard in an instant, which causes him to lick his lips. Despite taking my time, I'm soon standing naked in front of him.

He drags his eyes from my head to my toes and back again, finally resting on my very prominent erection.

"Utterly divine," he says huskily, and just his voice causes my cock to respond. He climbs off the bed and saunters over to me. He runs his hands down my torso and then, barely grazing across the one bit of me I want him to touch, cups my arse and pulls me towards him. I feel his robe drop open and he pulls me closer, pressing our cocks together between us. I shift a little to get a bit more friction.

"Dirty," he breathes. I'm not sure what he means—that I haven't had a shower yet, or that I'm trying to grind myself against him—but I don't care, as his voice does something to me.

"Dirty, dirty, dirty." His voice is guttural, and fuck, if he carries on in that tone, I might just come before we make it to the shower.

He leans close and inhales deeply, an action that has me even more aroused.

"I should see you after work more often if you smell this good." He inhales again, as if savouring an expensive scent.

"But, much as I'm enjoying this, I want to get you under that shower."

He releases his hold, and I lose the friction I had. But I'm not given time to lament its loss as he leads me to the bathroom.

I hadn't seen this room before, and now that I have I want to shower in here all the time. It's a bespoke cubicle with a huge overhead shower, along with a handheld unit and some directional body jets. At one end is a built-in stone bench, as it doubles as a steam room.

"You like it?" Duncan asks. He must have seen my eyes on stalks.

"I do." I can't answer anything more; I'm still taking it all in.

"Good," he says. "Because I've had one built into my house."

I didn't know that, and somehow the thought of visiting him seems even more attractive.

"Perhaps I can come and get dirty at your house, then." I say.

"Oh, I hope you're going to get *very* filthy."

Oh god, yes. I hope so, too.

He turns on the water and takes off his robe, hanging it on a hook next to its double.

"Now, let's get dirty together." He opens the door and pulls me inside.

He places me under the overhead shower and grabs some shower gel. He lathers his hands and washes me all over. His touch is slow and sensuous, and I relax into it, enjoying the feel of his hands running over my torso, across my shoulders, down my back and softly kneading my arse. He kneels down and soaps my legs, giving a teasing, light touch across my balls and up my crack. My breath hitches in anticipation of more.

"Sit." He gestures to the seat and I obey. Next, he grabs the shampoo and applies it to my hair. He's standing directly in front of me, and I can't help but reach out and suck his cock into my mouth. Having him massage suds into my scalp, while rhythmically filling my mouth with his cock, is nearly enough to make me come without him even touching me.

"God, that feels good, but not yet." He pulls out of my mouth and takes a step away, pulling me upright to rinse my hair.

He steps closer, one hand languidly playing up and down my length as he cups the nape of my neck, and we kiss. His tongue runs over my lips, and I let out a little whine. I feel him smile against my mouth, but I feel no shame at what his touch can do to me; I trust him completely.

"Turn round. Hands against the wall."

I do as he says, and he uses his foot to push my legs further apart.

"Are you okay?" he asks.

"I'm good," I assure him.

"If you want to stop at any point, just let me know."

"I will." I'm intrigued by what he has in mind.

Then he moves the directional body jets to play on my shoulders, ribs, and legs, turning the intensity up to full. It's fierce and I drop my head forward, losing myself to the force. I'm deprived of my other senses, and nothing else exists outside of this moment, this shower, and Duncan's touch. I don't know where he is until I feel a warm wetness against my hole.

"Fuck," I growl, as his tongue teases me. I push back, wanting more, and feel him probe into me, darting his tongue and lapping at me. I try to control my breathing to prevent losing it and nearly fail when he adds his teeth, nipping at my

161

pucker. It's only him laying a hand on my lower back that steadies me and keeps me grounded.

He runs his tongue lower and slurps one of my balls into his mouth, and I swear I stop breathing. I almost come with relief when a lubed finger breaches me, sliding in and out.

"More . . . please," I pant in desperation, and he adds another finger, lightly brushing across my gland again and again until I'm almost delirious. Then he withdraws his fingers and I whimper, my hole clenching round nothing. I feel his cock pushing against my entrance, and I unashamedly utter, "Yes, yes, yes," until I feel him filling me.

"I love seeing you so needy for me," he breathes against my back as he rocks his hips. He thrusts into me, and I've never felt so complete as when he's buried in me. Never so alive as when he's bringing me to the edge of oblivion. He places one foot on the stone bench, and the slight change in angle causes him to nail my gland.

"I can't hold on any longer, Dunc," I gasp, feeling the familiar and delectable tingling down my spine.

"Not yet, my love," he says soothingly, and slows his rhythm slightly. One hand fists my cock while the other snakes round my neck. He pulls me upright, plastering my back to his chest. The hand on my neck tightens to hold me in place. I can breathe, but only just, and I change to shallow breathing until I start feeling dizzy.

"You still okay, baby?" he asks, and I nod. I'm good—more than good.

I sag against him slightly, feeling a little unsteady on my feet.

"It's okay, I've got you." He presses his chest more firmly against me, lending support.

"You want to come for me?" he husks, and I nod again.

He pumps my cock faster, sliding his hand up over the tip each time.

"Come for me," he repeats, increasing his thrusts until I arch into his fist, and spill all over my chest and his hand. He releases my neck and I'm able to swallow again.

"Put your hands on the bench," he instructs, and I bend over, pushing my arse further into him.

"God Harlen, you feel so good." He grabs my hips and thrusts a few more times before I feel him come inside me.

He slowly pulls out and I turn, grateful I can sink down to sit on the bench. Duncan plops down next to me, leaning his forearms on his knees, panting.

"I wish I was twenty years younger." He chuckles, and I put a hand on his back, rubbing gently.

"I guess we could have some supports made for when we can't stand up anymore."

He laughs loudly and then turns to me, his face turning to concern. He holds my chin gently, turning my head and looking at my neck. "Are you okay? Did I hurt you?"

"No, I'm fine, and it was fucking awesome . . . though at my age I might need a minute or two before trying it again."

He laughs again and stands, turning off the body jets and inviting me to join him under the regular shower.

"Come on, let's get cleaned up again."

CHAPTER 34

 uncan

"Hı Dad, how's everything going?"

"It's all good," I reassure Jackson over the video call. I'm happy to see his face even though it's only been a week or so.

We're in the kitchen having breakfast, and Harlen passes me a cup of coffee. He leans in a little so he can see the screen and greets Jackson. I catch Jackson's smirk as he figures out that Harlen has probably stayed the night. I'm not giving anything away, though, and certainly not any details. I try not to think about it. It's totally inappropriate to think about how good your boyfriend's arse tastes as you video call your son. That doesn't really stop me though, and I zone out for a while, as they chat for a few minutes about the work on the trees.

"Dad! . . . Dad!" My attention is brought back to the present when Harlen nudges me, and I focus on the screen before Jackson calls out again.

"Where were you?" he asks, and then follows with, "No,

don't tell me that. I don't need to know." I can tell by the merriment in his eyes that he's noticed my blush. I also need to shift slightly to adjust how uncomfortable my thickening cock feels pressed against my trousers. Which does nothing to stop him chuckling at me. I groan inwardly; this is too much.

"I need to run a few errands and then go grab my tools," Harlen interjects, and I'm grateful for it. Then he stands behind me and tips my head back for a kiss. His hair falls over my face, so I'm pretty sure that Jackson doesn't see the saucy wink he gives me. One that tells me he knows exactly what I'd been thinking of. "See you later," he murmurs, low and quiet so only I can hear. But it's so gravelly that it travels straight to my balls. If I wasn't on a long distance video call with my family, there would be no way he'd be leaving this house without some sort of repeat performance of last night. I adjust myself again, and this time I'm treated to twin smirks—from Harlen, and from Jackson on-screen.

"Bye Jackson. Speak soon," he calls out, and Jackson answers with his goodbyes, too. When he's gone, I can see Jackson bursting to ask a bunch of questions.

"So is it going well?" He beams. "All domestic bliss?"

"Wait. Don't tell me that you fabricated a trip to the other side of the world just to give us a trial at living together?"

"Well, it wasn't my *only* reason," he laughs. He never ceases to surprise me. I didn't think him capable of that much cunning, though I know someone who is.

"Your sister." I groan, and I can tell by the look on his face that I've hit the nail on the head. I need to change the subject. I don't need my children interfering any more in my life. Though, to be fair, this experiment that they've conjured up is working out very well. And I'm hoping I can persuade Harlen to agree to the option of living with me, at least for some of the time.

I hear laughter behind Jackson and I'm grateful.

"Are you having a good time?" I ask, as it certainly sounds like it.

"Yes. I wish I'd tried to find Isabel sooner." His face darkens for a moment and I can see he's thinking about the reasons why this didn't happen. "But she's amazing, and she and Luca get on famously." I smile, as I knew that would happen. "And Gavin is a great guy."

"He sure is." I couldn't wish for a finer partner for my daughter, or someone to trust my business with.

Just then, the phone wobbles and I hear, "Uncle Jackson."

Jackson's face comes back into view with a beaming smile. He moves the phone and I see Scott has attached himself to Jackson's leg. I choke a little at seeing my precious grandson. I'm missing my grandchildren a lot, and know I'll have to go back soon just to see them.

Jackson crouches down next to him so I can see them both in the picture.

"Hey Scott!" I call, and he looks round.

"Grandaddy!" He looks elated, and my heart melts a little.

"How are you doing, buddy?" I ask him, and he gives it the serious contemplation that only a five-year-old can.

"I wish I had long hair like Jane," he answers eventually. Not what I was expecting, but I roll with it.

"Why's that?"

"Cos Uncle Luca made it look nice."

I can see the laughter Jackson is suppressing and raise an eyebrow. He answers.

"Luca braided Jane's hair, and now Scott wants his to look the same." He ruffles Scott's hair as if it's the most natural thing in the world. I feel a sharp pang that he hasn't experienced the joy of children. For whatever has happened in my life, I would never have given up the opportunity to be a father.

"Well, I'm sure it'll be long enough soon, buddy," I tell Scott.

But the next thought has entered his head, and he's suddenly out of shot, running to whatever has grabbed his attention.

Jackson stands again, but not before I catch the wistful look in his eyes.

"Hi Dad." Jackson turns the phone and I see Isabel, with Scott hoisted on her hip. "I need to get these terrors to bed. It's past their bedtime, but for some reason, having their uncles here makes them think every day is a holiday. Speak soon." Then she's gone in a whirlwind. I talk to Jackson for a bit longer and then we sign off, with the promise to talk again in a few days.

I check the clock. I have just enough time to get to the garage and give Pete the keys to Lilac Cottage before I need to be up at the house site. I just need to collect the last of my things. Not that there was much to start with, as I had nothing when I came over from Australia.

"THANKS, Pete. I appreciate you letting me rent it for a while."

"It does it good to be lived in," he says, taking the keys in. "Your new house ready, then?"

"Nearly. Just a couple of jobs left to do. I should be moving in within a couple of weeks."

"I heard it's right fancy." Pete sniffs. It isn't very fancy, but, well, it kind of is. Just not in an ostentatious way. I make a mental note to have a housewarming slash open house–style party when I've moved in.

"It's not really grand, and it certainly isn't as cosy as your cottage." That seems to please him. Just then, a figure comes out from the garage, dressed in oil-stained overalls, and slowly crosses the forecourt. He's huge. A bear of a man, easily six feet four and well-built. He has thick brown hair tied back, a beard, and kind grey eyes. If it wasn't for his hair colouring, I would almost say he was Keith's twin. Not that the village needs two Keiths. He's holding something in his large, paw-like hands.

"Pete, I think I've found the problem . . . Oh sorry," he says when he sees me.

"No problem, I'm going anyway."

"This here is Madsen." Pete waves him over.

"Pleased to meet you, Madsen." I hope he doesn't notice my lack of manners by not offering him my hand, but from the look of the amount of grease over his hands, I'd rather not.

"Err, hello," he says.

"Madsen," Pete continues. "I have the keys to the cottage, so you can move in whenever you want to now."

"Thanks Pete." A gentle smile crosses his face, and then he turns and ambles back to the garage.

"He's settling in well," Pete says, staring after him. "In some ways, he's a better mechanic than Charley; slower, but methodical. Charley can be impetuous sometimes, and I know that cars aren't his first love. It was always the horses with him. I still see him mind, when the family gets together, but I'm happy for him now."

I didn't want to interrupt Pete's speech, as I'd only met his nephew Charley once, when I took the cottage. But there's something nice about being accepted into a community enough that they assume you know who everyone else is—a sense of belonging. I'd been close to the centre of the village whilst renting the cottage, and I want to make sure that I don't lose that community feeling living out in my corner of the woods. I say my goodbyes and head up to the valley house.

I pull into the drive, and all the construction vehicles have gone now. The disruption they made is being put right, and the new grass and meadow species will start growing soon enough. All that's left now are the interior fitters, and I'm excited to see what the progress is.

My phone beeps in my pocket. It's Harlen, and happy as I am to speak to him, I wasn't expecting a call. I answer.

"Dunc." I can hear the anguish in his voice and all my senses ping to red alert.

"What is it, love?"

"My cabin, it's . . . it's on fire."

CHAPTER 35

arlen

I WATCH as the workshop collapses in front of me, the flames engulfing it billowing up into the sky and singeing the trees. Everything is just gone, in an instant.

I'd seen the smoke as I'd driven up to the cabin, but as soon as I arrived and saw how bad it was, I put in a nine-nine-nine call straight away, and then one to Duncan.

The fire brigade didn't try to save the workshop. Instead they're focussing on containing the fire and making sure it doesn't spread to the forest. They're soaking the surrounding trees, but letting the workshop burn for now. I don't blame them; forest fires can spread dangerously quickly. It has always been a risk, living in the woods like this, but I've always been so careful. I don't know what happened this time and I'm cursing myself for not being here to prevent it, though a tiny voice inside me says that it would probably have been futile. But this feeling of helplessness—like, if I could have just done something different I would have been able to change it all—is strong and won't go away.

The fire has already spread to the cabin, and flames are dancing across the corner. I'm told another crew is on their way to deal with it. All I can do is just sit and watch my life burn. I look towards the cabin and it doesn't look so bad right now. If the other fire crew gets here soon, they could save it, and I can rebuild what needs to be done. There is something I *do* want, though. I glance at the fire crew, but they're all occupied, and so I head towards the cabin before they can stop me.

When I open the door I hear a *whoosh,* and the flames at the far end burst up. A surging wave of smoke rolls towards me and I cover my mouth and nose. I hear a shout behind me, but ignore it. I'll only be a minute.

I make it across the room to the reading nook I have. The smoke is thicker and my eyes start stinging, so I close them. I feel along the shelf and close my fingers around the carving. I turn to go but suddenly feel disorientated. I press forward and feel my way along the room. I know it isn't far but it feels a million miles. I can't go on and fall to my knees, crawling along. My senses dull, and then I feel nothing.

BEEP, whoosh, beep, whoosh.

I slowly open my eyes into a gloomy room. They still hurt, but at least it isn't too bright. The only sound is the hum and beep of machines. A hospital room. I have a tube clipped to my nose and a small device attached to my finger. I start to recall what happened. *What was I thinking, entering a burning building like that?* I know better than that. It was stupid, I know that. Then I remember what I saved. I frantically look around for my things and can't see anything. There's a unit next to the bed, and I open the door on the front and peer in. I breathe a sigh of relief. It's there. They must have emptied my pockets. I reach in and pick it up, my fingers falling into the familiar grooves and indentations. To some it wouldn't mean anything, and it isn't much to look at, this small wooden giraffe. But to me it's the last link to my father, and the reason I went into woodworking. It's been my most treasured possession since he made it for me when I was seven years old. He made me a whole ark, a complete ship with pairs of animals, but most of them were lost years ago.

The giraffe was only saved as it was the piece I had been clutching when the car I'd been travelling in—and that my father had been driving—had been hit by a truck when I was nine. I lost both my parents that day, and I was lucky to survive, though I didn't feel lucky at the time. I haven't felt lucky for a long time; until recently that is. The door opens, bringing with it the light from outside, and I squint at the brilliance of it. A doctor appears in my vision.

"How are you feeling, Mr Davies?" He seems so cheerful.

"Okay, I guess." How am I supposed to feel? I've lost everything I built over the last twenty years.

He checks the readout from the device on my finger. "That looks good. You can stop the oxygen now, and we'll see how it goes." He points to my nose and I remove the cannula. He reaches over and switches a dial on the wall behind me. He watches the readout again for a while and gives an approving hum.

"Have you been coughing?" he asks.

"I haven't so far."

"Good. I think you got away lightly considering how much smoke you inhaled. Do you feel sick at all?"

"No, I feel okay."

"What about your eyes?"

"They sting a little, and the light is a bit bright."

"Let me have a look." He comes closer, lifting one eyelid at a time to shine a light into them. "I think it'll just be some drops for a few days and they'll be just fine. You were lucky." There's that word again. "I'll go and sort out a prescription and hopefully we can get you discharged soon. You might feel a bit short of breath for a few days, but you're pretty fit for your age, so I think you'll be okay. Take it easy for a while. If you develop a persistent cough, then go see your usual doctor."

He exits, leaving the door open. Noise filters in from outside, and I can hear the hustle and bustle of the rest of the ward. I can just see the corridor outside and make out the edge of the nurses' station, but not all of it.

I must have drifted off a little, as I come to with a voice I do recognise.

"Which room is he in?" The voice is dripping with fear.

"We only allow family outside visiting hours, sir. If you come back—"

"I am family. I'm his husband." My breath catches at what he says but I don't hear any more, as within seconds I'm smothered by him. My Duncan. He pulls back and then looks at me, his face furrowed with anxiety.

"Are you okay, my love? I was so worried about you. I tried to get here quicker, but by the time I got to the cabin you'd been taken away. I can't quite go as fast as an ambulance with its blue-and-twos on, especially not in the school rush." He stops for breath and strokes my hair away from my face. I love that gesture and endeavour to keep my hair long just so he can do that.

"What did you call me? Out there?" I nod towards the door. I see him thinking and then he smiles.

"I called you my husband. I'm sorry, I didn't think. I just wanted to make sure they let me in."

"It's okay, I—I kind of liked it."

I can't see his eyes in the darkened room, but I can see his expression tighten. "Do you mean that if I were to ask you to marry me, you'd say yes?" he whispers. I hear the hope—and the fear—in his voice.

It's not a proposal, except it sort of is, and faced with it, I actually don't know. I know there is no one I'd rather be with than Duncan, but it's a big step to take, and I don't think I'm ready for it yet. I'm not sure he's ready for the mess that is me, for all that he doesn't seem to mind it. I've also just lost my house and, for now, my livelihood, as I lost all my tools in the fire. I don't want to become a burden to anyone. I realise he's waiting for an answer whilst I internalise everything.

"Can I think about it?" I don't think it was the answer he was hoping for, but it's all I can give right now. I need to sort my life out first.

"Of course you can, love." He doesn't show any reproof, just the calm patience that is his way, and one of the many reasons I love him. "Now, tell me what the doctors have said."

I tell him I'm fine, that it was just a precaution, and I can go home soon.

In the end, it was another three hours before we could leave.

CHAPTER 36

uncan

I USHER Harlen into the living room at Larchdown House, and make him sit down on the couch and rest. He protests, of course, but he looks tired. I go to fetch him a coffee and when I return I can see his eyes are closed. I watch him for a few minutes, wondering how to proceed. While we've been living here for the past couple of weeks, I've spent some time trying to work out how to ask him to move in with me once my house is completed.

Every time I think it's the right moment, something seems to happen to spoil it, though I know that's just me making excuses and I'm a coward. I know how fiercely independent he is, and I know how he craves and needs his own space. But now he doesn't have his cabin, and it feels wrong to ask him, as if I'm taking advantage of the situation.

"Are you going to stand there all day or give me my coffee

before it gets cold?" He startles me from my pondering and I nearly drop the mug.

"I thought you were asleep."

"I was just resting my eyes."

"Oh, sorry. Do they still hurt?" I hand him the mug as he cracks an eye open and stares at me.

"C'mon, out with it."

"Out with what?" I ask, trying to show cool indifference.

"You're hovering there like a kid outside the headmaster's office. What is it?"

I sigh and sit down next to him. I guess I just need to get it over with.

"I've been wanting to ask you this for a while, but it just seems wrong now."

That gets me his full attention. "Ask me what?"

"Would you move into the valley house with me when it's finished?" I hold my breath, ready to try to counter his excuses.

"Yes." He takes a sip of his coffee like he was answering a question about whether he wanted butter on his toast. I gape at him.

He gives a little smirk. "Not the answer you were expecting, huh?"

"Well, no. If I'm honest, it's not."

"Yesterday it might have been a different answer, but right now I figure I don't have many options. So yes. But it will only be until I get back on my feet. Do you understand?"

"Yes, sure." I don't . . . well, I kind of do, and I don't like it. However, I'll take anything right now. I can work on the rest later.

"And you're not so difficult to live with." He laughs, but it turns into a coughing fit, and I take the mug from him and ease him back so he's lying down.

He closes his eyes again, and I see within a few minutes that he's asleep this time. I let him rest.

. . .

WHEN HE WAKES up a few hours later, and has eaten the soup I've made him, he looks much better, and a lot stronger.

I sit next to him on the couch and he snuggles into me. I definitely like having him this close and hope it'll be a regular thing. I put on an old film and settle down to watch it.

I am curious about one thing, but I didn't want to ask him at the hospital.

"What were you doing in the cabin? Why did you go in there? What were you thinking?" I try to keep the worry from my voice, but fail.

"I know it was stupid, but at that point the flames weren't too bad and I thought I had enough time."

"Time for what?" There can't have been anything in there that was worth risking his life over.

"In my jacket pocket."

"What?" I wonder if he's suddenly gone mad.

"Just fetch my jacket, please?"

"Fine." I get up and go out, coming back with his jacket and handing it to him. It smells of smoke, and I vow to stick it in the utility room and wash it tomorrow before it stinks the house up.

He hands me a wooden toy. I recognise it instantly. I understand why he wanted it. It doesn't excuse him putting his life in danger, but I get it. I sit down next to him, running my fingers over the little giraffe. I remember how this used to stand on his bookcase in his flat at uni. How he had to take it with him as a mascot into exams—his lucky charm, he called it. I also remember when he first told me the story of his parents. I hated how his life had been ripped apart so young and he'd had to live with his aunt, even though she did the best she could. But I used to love hearing him tell how he got the giraffe, and the memories he had of his family.

177

I look over and see him anxiously watching me. He is the bravest man I know. I go to give it back to him, and as his hand closes on mine, I pull him towards me and spin us round so we're lying lengthways on the couch. It brings back a deeply forgotten memory of how we occasionally used to lie like this, side by side on his couch, and I smile at the thought. Best friends indeed. Who was I kidding? I just hadn't worked out who I was at that time. Now, though, I have my arm round him and I know who I am, and who I want.

I lift up the hand holding the giraffe.

"Please tell me the story again?" I ask.

CHAPTER 37

 arlen

WE STAND at the edge of the wreckage; the remnants of what used to be my life. It's a mess. Blackened and twisted timbers reach skywards. A few of the trees have been badly scorched and in time I'll probably have to take them down, before they fall down.

My equipment is nothing but fire and water damaged lumps of metal, and the ashes of what was once my workshop settle round it like snow..

The cabin is half-burnt and the rest soggy. One wall has gone, and I can see straight into it. It feels odd being on the outside, looking in at my home like this. I feel detached from it, like I'm looking at someone else's life. I guess I'm still trying to process what happened.

There's still a crew on site, as they have to stay until they're sure the fire isn't going to start up again. Even one remaining ember in a wooden building could be enough to spark it off.

But they have soaked everything thoroughly. Once the crew is sure the fire will not reignite, the insurance company will come and take a look. Of course, everything was insured and I can replace the tools and the cabin, but the question remains: do I want to?

A fire officer makes his way over to us and introduces himself as an investigator.

"I think it was started by an electrical fault in the workshop."

"But there was nothing—" I was going to say that there was nothing on in the workshop, but then I remembered I had plugged in all my chargers that evening.

"I had some battery chargers plugged in; they're supposed to switch off when the battery is done charging."

"That could have been it." He nods. "It does happen if they're faulty. I still have a few things to look at, but you'll get my report as soon as I'm finished. I'll send a copy to your insurance company, too." He gives me his card so I can send him all the details, and heads back to dig about in the debris.

"How are you feeling?" Duncan asks, after the investigator is out of earshot. I shrug. I still don't know what to think. Actually I do, I just don't know if I can allow myself to feel this. But I think it's finally time to let go of the handrail.

I've had time to think since the fire and have come to some decisions. Once my tools have been replaced, I'll go back to my tree-surgeon work, but scale it back a bit to just the oldest clients, friends, and family. I thought I had ten years left in me before it became too much, but it seems better to just do less of it now. Edward from my therapy group has talked to me about a community project he would like help with and I want to concentrate more on the carving; I enjoy it. I'm trying not to mourn the pieces I lost in the fire. I can make those again, and maybe I'll consider carving a few bespoke pieces for people, like Duncan suggested. Damn him for being right as usual, but

I can't be angry with him as he always seems to have my best interests at heart.

I don't know if I'll rebuild the cabin. It took a lot of work, and I was a lot younger back then. But if I do, then I won't live in it. I might rent it out or offer it as a holiday let. I like Duncan's offer of staying with him in his gorgeous house and could live there quite happily with him.

"If this had happened a few months ago, I think I would have been devastated. I probably would have crawled into a hole and never left."

I see the anguish in his face, and I know what he's thinking. He could be right; it might have been the thing to tip me over the edge. But now everything is different, and I have to let him know that it's because of him.

"Now, somehow, it feels like the chance for a new beginning. A start over." I give him a smile and he mirrors it back at my choice of words.

"I know I'm homeless, and can't work for a while, but I have something more important than that. I have you Duncan. You've shown me that there is a life outside of myself. I can't promise that I'll always be able to engage in it, but I *will* try. You've shown me a future I never thought could exist and I'm forever grateful for that."

He turns towards me, and as he takes a step forward, he knocks something with his foot. Frowning with curiosity, he picks it up. It's the caged heart I'd made when he'd first arrived. He turns it over in his hands.

"I made that the weekend I first saw you again. It was the only way I could cope." My voice cracks, and he looks up from the carving at me, his eyes shining.

"Harlen. It's exquisite."

"May I?" I ask softly, reaching to take the carving from him. He relinquishes it to me. I drop it to the floor and put my foot on it.

"Wha—" I place a hand on Duncan's chest to stop him moving, as I press down with my foot until I hear a crack. Picking up the carving, I pull apart the pillars of the cage I'd snapped and tease out the heart in the middle. I throw the cage towards the rubble of my house and turn back to Duncan. I take his hand and place the wooden heart in the middle of his palm, folding his fingers over it.

"It's yours now. Will you look after it for me?"

"Forever." He says before pulling me to him, the heart in our hands crushed between us as he kisses me.

CHAPTER 38

$\mathcal{H}$arlen

I STAND at the window of the valley house and watch leaves of burnished gold flutter on their journey to the valley floor. The trees are entering a cycle of slumber followed by renewal in the spring, a period of regrowth and rebirth. We've been living here for a few weeks, and some days it feels like I've always lived here, like it's always been my home. I know I'd told Duncan I would stay until I got back on my feet, but in truth, I don't want to leave. We're repurposing a building that was earmarked as a sauna and gym as a workshop for me, with a room to sleep in if I need to; my cabin in miniature. I'm going to rebuild the cabin house, but will rent it out either to long-term tenants or as a holiday house. I think about how my life has changed over the last few months, and how I feel peaceful and more at ease. I turn and look over at the man who made it possible. Who believed in me enough that I could believe in myself. I no longer have regrets about the past. If we'd been together for thirty years, things might have been different, but I relish the chance of thirty years with him now—and I also know I can finally answer his question.

Not yet, though. Not until the guests have all departed. The open housewarming event has been a huge success. The villagers have all had a chance to *oooh* and *aaah* at this magnificent house, and I feel lucky to have the opportunity to live in it. Although it isn't made of wood, I feel as close to the forest as I would if I was in my cabin. Almost more so, as the floor-to-ceiling glass in this section has me amongst the trees. I feel like I can almost reach out and touch them. We watched a deer move through the trees as we were eating breakfast this morning and I don't know who had the biggest grin. I'd teased Duncan, that I bet he didn't have these sights in his fancy-pants Sydney apartment.

The main living floor is an open-plan, wedge-shaped space with a seating area in one front corner. A fire pit separates it from a dining area in the other front corner. Behind these is a kitchen space and more seating. Downstairs are a couple of bedrooms, with an ensuite and a movie den. Upstairs are more bedrooms, a library, and an office space. Every room has gorgeous views out into the woods and across the valley to the downs.

I'm joined at the window by Keith, who watches the leaves falling for a few minutes before he speaks. "It's been a funny old time for you, hasn't it?"

"You could say that." I huff a laugh. It's the understatement of the year.

"Ah well, sooner or later things in Larchdown have a habit of sorting themselves out. We just have to catch the right turning of the seasons."

"Has it been my season, then?"

"Aye, that it has." He pauses. "Now come and show me round this marvellous house of yours."

"Duncan's house."

"Stop kidding yourself. He built it for you."

I stare after him as he strides across the room, and the last few pieces of a puzzle I didn't know I was constructing fell into place. I think of the building set a little way up the hill. A building that he . . .

I corner Duncan in the kitchen area and stand in front of him.

"There never was going to be a gym and sauna house, was there?"

He shrugs and smirks at me.

"You sneaky, conniving, manipulative, *ngngng*." He silences me with a smouldering kiss that leaves me a little breathless.

"You know it turns me on when you talk to me like that and I can't keep my hands off you," he says, his lips just millimetres from my own as he pulls my hand to his crotch to emphasise the point. I can feel his hot length straining in his trousers. "So unless you want to flash these guests your arse when I bend you over the counter, can we save it until later?"

"Mmm, I can wait." I kiss him, adding a nip to his lip that lets him know we will return to this subject. He growls into my mouth and I nearly forget we have guests at all.

"But also, thank you," I add, and he gives me his beautiful smile before I jog to catch up with Keith and show him the rest of the house.

Why had he never told me he'd included me in his plans? But I know the answer—because I would never have believed him, and would've refused to let him do it. But he did it anyway, and I know I don't deserve someone as wonderful as Duncan Blake.

When we arrive back in the main living space, Duncan is saying goodbye to the last few guests. Because he is also an astute and successful businessman, he'd invited Holly Vance and Kayla Brown from the contractor's company, as well as some of his own clients, using the event to showcase his work.

He should be proud of it. I'm looking forward to when my new workshop is ready and I can start making some furniture, including carving a new headboard for the enormous bed we've had installed. *We!* Keith's words have been infused into my soul and now that I'm thinking of us for the house, there's another type of *us* I want to think about.

Finally, the only people left are Jackson and Luca. I head over to the large corner seating by the window and sit down, enjoying a view I will never tire of.

Duncan comes over and sits next to me. I turn to him.

"My answer is yes."

He looks puzzled. "And the question was?"

"If you ask me to marry you, the answer will be yes."

"What's going on?" Jackson asks, as both he and Luca flop onto the couch opposite.

"Harlen's just said he'll marry me."

"Wait, hold on," I protest. "I did not say that. I said that if you asked me, I would say yes. You haven't asked me yet."

"Good luck there." Luca grins. "It must be a Blake thing. I believe my proposal was half-arsed as well."

"Hey!" Jackson calls. "I'm not sure I like this ganging up on the Blakes." But there's no heat to his protest.

Duncan leans close, so only I can hear, and murmurs, "You play a dangerous game." That voice, as always, snakes down my spine and wraps itself around my balls, and I know later I'm going to be the one begging him to marry me as he controls my pleasure with his fingertips. I can't fucking wait, and even thinking about it is making me feel lightheaded.

"So can I call you both Dad now?" Luca asks cheekily, and I instinctively move to say no. But I'm stopped by the sight of Jackson, doubled over laughing, like he knew this would happen.

"It might take some getting used to, but I guess it would be okay." I'm still not sure if it's the right thing to do, but it seems to make Luca happy. And I have to admit it makes me feel, well, like part of the family.

Jackson manages to stop laughing and instead takes Luca's hand.

"Well, seeing as you haven't asked, and you haven't said yes." He indicates to Duncan and myself in turn. "Can we tell you our news instead?"

"Of course," Duncan replies.

"Well." Jackson takes a deep breath, and I feel Duncan press his thigh alongside mine, as if he's worried about what he's going to hear and wants to stay in contact with me. I press back my support.

"We didn't want to tell you yet, until we'd sorted out the details. It's something we've been thinking about for a while now, but it wasn't until we went to Australia that the solution was provided. By Isabel."

He pauses, and I can feel Duncan tense up beside me.

"We want to be parents."

Duncan erupts and grabs Jackson for the biggest hug I've ever seen. Tears stream down his face. He envelops Luca into the embrace and then grabs me to join in. When he can start making coherent sounds, he lets us go.

"I am so fucking happy for you. Tell me all—how and why—and what Isabel has to do with it."

Jackson puts his arm around Luca and holds him close.

"We've been talking about it for a while, even before we got married, in fact. Neither of us had the best upbringing." He halts whatever Duncan was about to say. "No Dad, we know where the fault lies there. But Luca especially, and we would like the chance to have our own and give them a good childhood. We didn't know how to go about it, but when we spoke to Isabel, she offered to be a surrogate for us."

I chance a look at Duncan, and I think he's about to explode with pride. I grab his hand and give it a squeeze. He gives me a grateful smile.

"We needed to sort out things legally, which we did as soon as we got back, but in the new year we'll be going back to Australia to start the process."

I've rarely seen Duncan lost for words, but he seems so now. He grabs Jackson and plants a massive kiss on his forehead, and the same to Luca, and then we're all hugging again.

"I know you're going to be the best parents ever," he tells them over and over, and eventually they're allowed to leave, and all is quiet again.

Darkness is falling, and I stand at the window watching the shadows deepen. I'm still processing Jackson and Luca's news, but I'm really happy for both of them. And for Duncan. He comes to stand behind me, his arms encircling me as he rests his head on my shoulder.

"A grandfather again, eh?" I ask softly.

"Yes. And you're going to be an amazing grandfather, too." His breath on my neck is sending goosebumps across my skin.

"Oh, I don't know about that. I haven't even been a father."

"Don't worry, I'll be there every step of the way." He presses a kiss below my ear and I shiver slightly, nerve endings tingling.

"Will you teach me everything?"

"Everything." The low rumble travels straight to my cock, my blood flow with it, and my trousers feel too tight.

"Well," I say slowly.

"What is it?" Another hot kiss burns my skin.

"I don't think I can do any of that."

"And why's that?" He nuzzles into my neck, and my knees nearly buckle.

"Because you haven't asked me to be part of your family

yet." This time I get the reaction I want as his teeth dig into the junction of my shoulder and neck.

"Fuck yeah!" My head swims in painful pleasure and I lean back further into him.

"Well, let's do something about that. You're going to be screaming "yes" before I've finished with you."

I'm definitely up for that. He takes my hand and leads me to our bedroom.

Not ready to leave the Valley yet?

Learning the Taste of Love is coming June 2024 but you can read the first chapter now:

Jacob

"Fuck!"

An electric shock pulses through my hand and up my arm. It isn't painful so much as a surprise. I jump back and snag my leg on a thorny bush. I pull myself free and with my balance never good at the best of times, I try to stop myself from falling. I grab the fence again, causing another jolt of electricity to travel up my arm. This time, when I stagger back I fall arse first into the prickly bush.

Fuck. My. Life.

I try to pull myself free—first one arm, then the other—but the thorns hold me fast and I can just *see* me dying here. It would be a fitting end. I wouldn't mind so much but it hurts like a bitch.

Cause of death: Can't get himself out of a shrubbery , or . . . Death by a thousand pricks.

Even in my predicament, I giggle to myself about the last one—that would certainly be a way to go, and obviously not these kinds of pricks—but it doesn't help, and if anything I'm even more stuck.

A shadow falls across me.

"Don't struggle, you'll make it worse. I'll come and help."

I might just have died and gone to Heaven, no wait, Valhalla as I look up and see the biggest fucking Viking ever.

"I don't need any help," I grumble. Certainly not by someone so perfectly proportioned and evenly featured as the guy in front of me. He even has the blonde locks, tied up into an alluring bun. He's holding on to a huge horse, and even that is peering at me curiously.

If I wanted to be rescued by a knight and his horse, I would want it to be from something more appropriate—such as being locked in a castle, or trapped under the spell of an evil witch—not the undignified position I find myself in.

He crosses his arms and gives me an amused smirk. "Okay then, I'll just watch and make sure you don't harm the bush."

"Harm it? It's fucking dangerous! It's like some sort of guard bush. There should be a warning on it." Now I've started I can't stop. "And that"—I gesture with my hand, as much as I can move it, towards the fence—"gave me an electric shock! I could have a heart condition. I could be dead by now."

"You do realise you're on private land, don't you?"

Of course, Mr perfect-looking Viking would point out that minor detail while I'm in full flow, wouldn't he?

"Well, there should be some laws about that."

"There are, and you aren't on the right side of them."

Well, that's shit.

"Look. I'll overlook the fact that you're trespassing if you tell me what you're doing out here."

Ha. No way. He's not getting anything from me. I'm not telling anyone my story.

"The drugs weren't working so I thought I'd try electric shock treatment."

He narrows his eyes for a few seconds and then tips his head back and laughs. A deep belly laugh, so loud even the horse takes a step away from him and tosses it's head.

Yeah, I'm with you there horse.

Eventually his laughing subsides and he looks at me, his eyes dancing.

"So, don't need any help then?" He's still smirking.

"I'm good. I'm just going to hang here for a bit."

"Okay, and when you're free, the quickest way to the main road is that way." He points over my right shoulder.

"Gotcha. Thanks." I nod, trying my best to look nonchalant, as if hanging around in bushes was a favourite pastime of mine.

"Okay. Well, bye then."

"Bye."

He turns round and starts walking along the fence line, the horse plodding along beside him.

I try to move my arm and I gain a few inches of movement—a-ha, I'm out of here. I try to tug my leg free but hear a ripping sound, and a sharp pain drags it's way down the back of my thigh. I do manage to get my foot on the ground, but as soon as I put some weight on it my knee buckles, and I end up back where I started—if not even more stuck. Fuck my disability. I sigh. It's clear I'm not going to get out of this thorny hell on my own.

"Erm, Mr Viking?" I call out, and watch him stop and slowly turn round.

"How are you doing?" he asks, still with that damn smirk.

"I was thinking that I could be off your land quicker if you'd give me a hand. Seeing as I'm, you know, trespassing."

He takes a minute, as if he's considering what I said before ambling back over.

"Okay, you've got yourself a deal."

He lets the horse go and tells it to stand, which—I'll be damned—it does. Then, he takes off his jacket and throws it across the electric fence before climbing over. Oh, that's how you do it. I file that information away for future use.

Once in front of me, his smirk is gone and he's all concern and concentration.

"Hold still," he instructs, and carefully pulls the thorny strands away from my right arm. Once it's free, he grabs my hand and holds it and me steady with one hand, while he starts to untangle my leg. I can see he's trying to be as gentle as possible, but still some thorns dig into my flesh, and I wince. He mutters, "Sorry," and tries to be more gentle.

"Can you stand?" he asks, once I have one leg free. I put my foot to the ground, but again it won't fully support me, so I cling to his shoulder as he untangles my other arm and leg. Judging by the draught I have wafting round my backside, there's been some extensive damage to my trousers. Which is just shit, as they're my only pair. Once I'm free, I let go of his shoulder, and he holds my hands until I feel steady enough to stand. I wobble a little but I'm not going to fall. I straighten up as tall as I can make myself, which is about up to the giant's shoulder.

"Well, thank you. I'll just be on my way now."

He frowns. "You can't go like that, you're bleeding."

I try to turn and look at my exposed thighs, and nearly overbalance. He catches hold of me before I crash back into the killer bush, and helps me stand again.

"Look. Come back with me to the farm, so we can get you cleaned up and find you some new trousers." He looks at me expectantly.

I hadn't wanted to meet anyone, though I *was* originally heading for the farm. I've found that remote farms and cottages are usually left unlocked, and I can often sneak in for a bit of food, or some clothing. But these scratches do hurt, and I can't go around with my arse hanging out. I'll get caught for indecent exposure, instead of just being thought of as a hobo as my clothes and unshaven face suggest. It's a good look. It means people leave me alone, which is what I want. I sigh. I'll get some trousers, and maybe I can sneak a bit of food and be on my way before he asks too many questions.

"Alright. I think it's the least you can do after your bush attacked me."

"Attacked you?"

"Did you not see it? It jumped straight up and ensnared me like some sort of sleeping-beauty hedge."

He helps me climb over the electric fence before retrieving his jacket.

"I guess you weren't the right prince for the princess then." He looks grave but his eyes hold amusement.

Yes, well, I'm not into princesses, so that analogy doesn't work. "I could have been the princess for all the bloody bush cared."

His mouth gives a slight quirk but he doesn't say anything. He just starts walking, collecting the horse's lead rein as he goes.

I follow on behind. I'm not a fast walker—too uncoordinated for that

—and after a few minutes he looks back with genuine concern on his face.

"Are you alright?"

I'm not about to explain my troubles, or my disability to him.

"I've just been maimed by your damn greenery, and been given two heart-stopping electric shocks. I'm doing the best I can," I snap. I'm also tired. I've walked several miles already today and I've not eaten since yesterday, so not at my strongest.

"I can put you up on Samson if you like." He gestures to the horse.

"Up there?" No way. It looks as high as a house, and I don't really know horses. I mean, they're okay—from afar. I'm already too close for comfort but Samson, as he called it, looks fairly docile despite being massive. But get on it? No, that isn't going to happen.

"I'll manage." I hurumph, and continue walking. He sighs and walks with me, this time keeping pace. It's slow going as I'm starting to get very sore from the scratches.

"So, what's your name?" he asks, breaking the silence after a few minutes.

The question catches me off guard. "J-John." I recover just in time.

"Well J-John."

"It's just John."

"Is it?"

"I know my own name."

"I'm sure you do," he replies, in a tone that says he knows very well I've given him a false name.

"Where are you heading?" he asks. So nosy.

"Oxford." I say the first thing that comes into my head. Well I am going in that direction, and Oxford is as good a place as any other. He nods, and thankfully doesn't ask any more questions I don't have the answer to.

"What's your name?" I might as well ask, though the less I know the better.

"Johan."

Oh, he is a proper Viking then. I thought he had a nice accent.

"And this is my brother-in-law's farm." We've reached a gate, that Johan opens onto a yard area surrounded by several buildings. There are a couple of vehicles parked up but I can't see anyone else about.

"Wait here," he says, and takes Samson over to another gate. After taking him through, he takes off the bridle and lets him go. He ambles off to join some other horses in the field.

"Now, come with me. Let's sort those scratches out." He leads the way to a small brick building across the yard and opens the door. It's a clean room, fitted out with cabinets and a central table. There are also some large cages along one side, and a sink on the opposite wall. He goes over to the cabinets and starts opening the doors, peering in. He takes a few things out and places them on the table in front of me. Taking a shallow, steel bowl he heads to the sink and half-fills it with water. Coming back to the table, he picks up a bottle and pours some pink gloop into the water, swirling it slightly to mix it.

"Okay, I think we're ready." He looks at me and then down at my ripped jeans. "I think you're going to have to take those off."

"I never drop my trousers on a first date." Who am I kidding?

He chuckles. "Well, can you make an exception?"

For you, my Viking, anything. Too bad I'd noticed the wedding band on his finger. Lucky, whoever she was. Not that I was wanting to start anything here. Get some clothes and move on, always moving on. Which is a shame, as it's been a long time since I've hooked up with anyone.

I slip out of my jeans and turn round, leaning my hands on the table.

Johan grabs a cloth and dips it in the water before crouching down behind me and applying it to the scratches. It stings and I can't help but flinch, but I withstand it and after a while it stops hurting so much.

After a couple of minutes, he hums. I don't know if it's a good noise or a bad one, so I ask.

"Are you checking out my arse down there Mr Viking?"

He just chuckles before standing up.

"Johan . . . Johan." A shout comes from outside, and he gives me a sheepish grin before a figure enters the room. What is this place? It's full of hot men. This guy is gorgeous—dark and brooding. He scowls at us, looking first at me, then at Johan, and then he looks at the table.

He crosses the space and picks up the bottle.

"Johan, what have you been doing?"

"John here got tangled up in a dog rose. I've been cleaning him up." His gaze swings back to me and takes in the fact that I'm without my trousers.

"How many times have I told you this stuff is for animals only?"

"It'll be fine," Johan protests.

The guy sighs and puts the bottle down. He turns his attention back to me.

"John, meet Cole, my husband. He's a vet." Johan introduces us. "Cole, this is John. Like I said, he had a fight with a bush."

Okay . . . Not a wife then, interesting. But too bad they're married. Stop it! Moving on, remember?

"Show me," Cole says, and he too crouches down behind me. My arse hasn't had so much attention in a long time.

"Can I touch it?" he asks, and I like that he shows respect.

"Yes, but I warn you I haven't been touched in a long time." That earns me another chuckle from Johan. But Cole doesn't say anything, he just lightly touches round the scratches, gently probing the skin.

He stands up. "They aren't too deep. They should heal okay. When did you last have your tetanus shot?"

"I don't know." I truly couldn't remember. "When I was a kid, perhaps."

"You should go get one."

"No, no doctors." There's no chance I'm going anywhere near a doctor or a hospital. No place anyone can trace me.

"Could you—"

"No Johan, I could not," Cole says sharply. "For a start, animal vaccinations are not the same as human ones, and I'd lose my license."

They turn back to me.

"I'm not going to see a doctor."

"We should do something," Johan says. "It was our bush that attacked him."

Cole thinks for a minute. "Okay, we won't take you to a doctor, *if* you agree to stay here for a few days so we can make sure you're okay and aren't going to get worse. And I'll find some human ointment for those scratches so they don't get infected."

I look from one to the other. I can't believe these strangers have helped me so much.

"Okay." I agree, but I've no intention of keeping to it. I'm on my way out of here as soon as I have something to wear and some food.

ALSO BY JEM WENDEL

Putting Down Roots - Larchdown Valley Book 1

https://books2read.com/puttingdownroots

Jackson

Jackson's plan had been a simple one—fill the van with fuel and drive until it ran dry, then start his life all over again.

Luca

Luca's art career is on the rocks after a spiteful review from his art critic ex-lover.

Bridging the Gap - Larchdown Valley Book 2 - Out Now

https://books2read.com/bridgingthegap

Cole:

I like my life the way it is—my job, having my family close, my animals—and contrary to what my brother thinks, I don't need to find love.

Johan:

Going to England was my chance to bury memories of my cheating ex while following one simple rule: no dating. Despite my best efforts, that rule goes out the window the second I lay eyes on Cole, the gorgeous, smart-as-hell vet of Larchdown Valley.

Will I only get my heart broken again? Or will Cole find he does want to share his life with someone, and that someone could be me?

ACKNOWLEDGMENTS

There are many people, without whom this book would not have been possible.

Special thanks to Hinsel for for sharing book ideas, reading everything first, supporting a fellow author, the daily chat and being my writing bestie. Thanks to JoJo and Rebecca for our support circle. To my lovely beta readers - Wren, Tanya, Steph and Jo. Thanks also to Steph for the feedback and stepping up to help support me. And to Jenn and SJ for making sure my words are all in the correct order. And last but definitely not least thank you to my husband for putting up with and supporting my crazy.

Stay in touch
https://www.instagram.com/jemwendelbooks
https://www.tiktok.com/@jemwendel
https://www.bookbub.com/authors/jem-wendel
https://www.facebook.com/jemwendelbooks
https://jemwendel.com

ABOUT THE AUTHOR

Jem Wendel is a British author who lives on the East Coast. She has been writing since she was old enough to hold a pen and has written several short stories as well as non-fiction articles for magazines and journals.

She specialises in M/M romances that are sweet, low angst with heat and a HEA.